Helen Garner was born in 1942 in Geelong, Victoria, and was educated there and at Melbourne University. She has worked as a high school teacher and freelance journalist. Her first novel, *Monkey Grip*, appeared in 1977. It won the National Book Council Award in 1978, and a feature film based on it was released in 1982. Her second book, *Honour & Other People's Children*, was published in 1980. She has received several fellowships from the Literature Board of the Australia Council, and has worked as writer-in-residence in Tokyo and at Griffith University and the University of Western Australia. She lives in Melbourne.

by the same author

MONKEY GRIP
HONOUR & OTHER PEOPLE'S CHILDREN

THE
CHILDREN'S
BACH

❖

HELEN GARNER

Published with the assistance of the
Literature Board of the Australia Council

McPHEE GRIBBLE/PENGUIN BOOKS

McPhee Gribble Publishers Pty Ltd
66 Cecil Street
Fitzroy, Victoria, 3065, Australia

Penguin Books Australia Ltd,
487 Maroondah Highway, P.O. Box 257
Ringwood, Victoria, 3134, Australia
Penguin Books Ltd,
Harmondsworth, Middlesex, England
Penguin Books,
40 West 23rd Street, New York, N.Y. 10010, U.S.A.
Penguin Books Canada Ltd,
2801 John Street, Markham, Ontario, Canada
Penguin Books (N.Z.) Ltd,
Private Bag, Takapuna, Auckland 9, New Zealand

First published by McPhee Gribble Publishers, 1984
This edition published by McPhee Gribble Publishers
in association with Penguin Books Australia, 1985
Reprinted 1985

Copyright © Helen Garner, 1984

Offset from the McPhee Gribble Publishers' edition
Made and printed in Australia by
The Dominion Press–Hedges & Bell

National Library of Australia
Cataloguing-in-Publication data
Garner, Helen, 1942- .
The children's Bach.
ISBN 0 14 008371 5.
I. Title.
A823'.3

2293437

For Alice and J-J, and for some very good
friends of mine.

This book is a work of fiction. Its characters
do not exist outside these pages.

Acknowledgment is made to Allans Music Australia Ltd for permission to quote from E. Harold Davies' introduction to the music book *The Children's Bach*.

The lines on page 86 are from *To Penshurst* by Ben Jonson.

I am happy to acknowledge the generous support given me by the Literature Board of the Australia Council during the year it took me to write this book. Some of it was written during a term I spent as writer-in-residence at Griffith University in Queensland.

DEXTER found, in a magazine, a photograph of the poet Tennyson, his wife and their two sons walking in the garden of their house on the Isle of Wight. To the modern eye it is a shocking picture: they are all, with the exception of the great man himself, bundled up in such enormous, incapacitating garments. Eye-lines: Tennyson looks into the middle distance. His wife, holding his arm and standing very close to his side, gazes up into his face. One boy holds his father's hand and looks up at him. The other boy holds his mother's, and looks into the camera with a weak, rueful expression. Behind them, out of focus, twinkles the windy foliage of a great garden. Their shadows fall across the lawn: they have just taken a step. Tennyson's hands are large square paws, held up awkwardly at stomach level. His wife's face is gaunt and her eyes are set in deep sockets. It is a photo of a family. The wind puffs out the huge stiff curved sleeve of the woman's dress, and brushes back off his forehead the long hair of the father's boy who is turned towards the drama of his parents' faces; though he is holding his father's hand, he is separate from the group, and light shows between his tightly buttoned torso and his father's leg.

Dexter stuck this picture up on the kitchen wall, between the stove and the bathroom door. It is torn and stained, and coated with a sheen of splattered cooking grease. It has been there a long time. It is always peeling off, swinging sideways, dangling by one corner. But always, before it quite falls off the wall, someone saves it, someone sticks it back.

❖

At night, when they had put the children to bed, Athena and Dexter walked. They were ruthless about going, and would barely even check that the boys were asleep before they set out. They gossiped and reported to each other the day's residue.

'See that house?' said Dexter. 'Outside there this morning,

on my way to work, I unwisely engaged in a conversation with a
senile know-all. I'm glad *you* think it's funny.'

Dexter walked with a bandy, rapid gait. They kept pace
easily, not touching. They covered miles each night in the
dark, sometimes heading east along the creek across the park-
lands to where it joined the Yarra River, sometimes northwest
as far as the huge upturned saucer of Royal Park where the
wild dogs in the zoo howled at the moon and monkeys gib-
bered behind the wall. Dexter pursed his lips and whistled a
curly tune. He was an old-fashioned joyful whistler who loved
merry trills, and as he approached the climax of the melody he
stopped walking, turned to Athena and raised one crooked
forefinger to alert her to his impending triumph.

'And now,' he announced at the crossroads outside a bank, 'I
shall sing the catalogue aria from *Don Giovanni*.' He had once
been told by an egalitarian friend of his father's that he had a
fine voice. He fancied himself a dramatic baritone in the
Russian style, but could also turn out a creditable version,
word-perfect, of 'The Vicar of Bray' or 'Jerusalem'. Dexter
wanted to live gloriously, and on the night walks he did,
making families turn from their screens, trumpeting through
the dreams of children, setting dogs to roar and scrabble
behind tin fences.

'You never sing!' he cried, all aglow, to Athena.

'Yes, I do,' she said, but he had already struck up another
chorus. She loved him. They loved each other. They were
friends. They lived in a sparsely furnished house near the
Merri Creek: its walls were cracking, its floors sloped and its
doors hung loosely in their frames. There was a piano in the
kitchen and during the day Athena would shut herself in there
under the portrait of Dexter's father and pick away at Bartok's
Mikrokosmos or the easiest of Bach's Small Preludes. Preludes to
what? Even under her ignorant fingers those simple chords
rang like a shout of triumph, and she would run to stick her hot
face out the window. There were days, though, when her
approach to the music, under the portrait with its yearning,
nineteenth century look, was so unrhythmic and lacking in
melody that she was ashamed, as if she had defaced an altar,
and she closed the piano and went out into the back yard with a
broom. Over the back fence, nearer the creek, lived an old

couple whom Dexter and Athena had never seen but whom they referred to as Mister and Missus Fuckin'. They drank, they smashed things, they hawked and swore and vomited, they cursed each other to hell and back.

❖

How strange it is that in a city the size of Melbourne it is possible for two people who have lived almost as sister and brother for five years as students to move away from each other without even saying goodbye, to conduct the ordinary business of their lives within a couple of miles of each other's daily rounds, and yet never to cross each other's paths. To marry, to have children; to fail at one thing and to take up another, to drink and dance in public places, to buy food in supermarkets and petrol at service stations, to read of the same murders in the same newspapers, to shiver in the same cold mornings, and yet never to bump into each other. Eighteen, twenty years may pass! How strange!

Had Dexter and Elizabeth thought of each other during this time? Of course they had, Dexter more than Elizabeth, not because of any imbalance of affection, but because Dexter was mad about the past. He believed in it, it sustained him, he used it to knit meaning into the mess of everything. He recited it in anecdotes always told in the same words. He even recalled in detail dreams that other people had had years before. Elizabeth disliked the past. It was full of embarrassment. She and Dexter had never been in love, but once she lay on his bed, in college, a whole Saturday afternoon waiting for him to come back because she wanted to fuck somebody and at the time there was no-one else. She lay there all hot and impatient for hours but he didn't come back and he didn't come back, and she got up and leaned out the narrow window, through which a warm wind was blowing, and she heard shouts from the university oval and realised he must be out there playing cricket. She got off the bed, straightened the blanket, and went back across the garden and through the gate to her own room in the next building. She was cross. And she never told him about it. The victories she scored against his voracious memory were small.

❖

In her wallet Elizabeth had a photo. On a bare wooden veran-dah stood a two-handled tartan overnight bag. The bag looked stable; it was packed solid. The top zip was undone. Out of it, between the two curved handles, stuck a child's head. The face looked straight at the camera, round and unsurprised. Its hair was tangled, its skin was dark, the whites of its eyes were bright white. On the back of the picture, in their mother's loose, frightening hand, were the words: 'Vicki: precious cargo'. Their mother had dropped her bundle, and died. What is possible between two sisters born twenty years apart? Is the elder one to be sister, or mother?

Elizabeth was sitting up in bed at one o'clock in the morning doing her crochet and watching 'Designing Woman' on TV. The telephone rang just as the dog was about to make its appearance carrying the husband's shoe. Elizabeth heard the pips.

'Vicki. Is anything wrong?'

'Not exactly.'

'What's the time over there?'

'Ten o'clock in the night.'

'I can't come over again,' said Elizabeth. 'I don't know why you're ringing me. The phone bill must be colossal. Have you been going to school?'

'Sort of. Not all that much.'

Elizabeth kicked the cooling hot water bottle off the end of the mattress. The top sheet was stolen, the bottom one paid for. They made a pair.

'You swore you were old enough to look after yourself. I warned you. I told you I couldn't keep on coming over. Do you know what that air fare costs?'

'I don't want you to come over,' said Vicki. Her voice was dull. 'I made a mistake. I want to come over there.'

'To *live*?'

'I'm only seventeen.'

'Last time we had this discussion, seventeen was adult, remember?'

The girl said nothing. The line hissed and sang. Their mother was dead and they were making a mess of things.

❖

Philip did not turn up with the car. This did not surprise Elizabeth. She took the bus to the airport. Vicki's plane was late.

Elizabeth walked up and down on the shiny tiles. She did not like people to observe that she was being kept waiting, and at least one girl was smiling at her in that shy, dawning way which meant she had seen Elizabeth on TV; but there was no decent coffee to be had, and no civilised place to sit. She measured her pulse on a tin machine outside the chemist shop. The reading she got was so low that she thought the thing must be out of order. She strolled into the shop, stole a twenty-five dollar Dior lipstick and a cheap plastic-covered address book and tried again: the adrenalin rush of petty theft showed. The address book would do for Vicki, if she hadn't missed the plane altogether. She transferred the stolen items from her sleeve to her bag and went into the cafeteria for a bottle of mineral water.

A man was sitting with his back to her, just inside the row of plastic potplants which fenced off the cafeteria. She had to narrow herself and slide sideways to get past his inconveniently placed chair. Which of her senses recognised him first? She

[5]

was close enough to smell his unwashed hair, to see the way his shirt collar stuck up stiffly round his ears, to hear the cheerful slurp of his mouth at the cup. She was right behind him, poised on her toes. Could it be? And if she spoke, would she be sorry afterwards?

'Excuse me,' she said.

He turned his head. It was Dexter.

Oh, her awful modern clothes, her hair spiked and in shock. He saw the fan of lines at the outer corner of her eye and his heart flipped like a fish. He pushed back his chair and stood up in a clumsy rush.

'Morty,' he whispered. 'Morty, look. It's me.'

'I thought it might be,' she said, 'I thought it was.' She heard the warmth go out of her voice and the dryness come in, and wanted to cry for something lost. Why isn't he roaring? Why isn't he making a fuss? Isn't he glad to see me? Don't I look all right? But we never used to hug. Why should we start now?

'You look very – you look –' He could not find a polite word, he was so full of feelings.

'That's the same coat,' she said, stepping back and pointing. 'The same smelly old khaki coat.'

'My father's here,' said Dexter. 'Look, Dad! It's Morty!'

Dexter's father had a paper serviette tucked into his collar and a fork in one hand. He moved his hat off the extra chair and dithered with it. Beside him sat a small boy with pale eyes and a Prince Valiant haircut. Dexter was recovering, was beginning to prance about in his great brogues with his arms out in a curve. Elizabeth slid past him and into the seat.

'I'll go for some cake!' shouted Dexter.

Doctor Fox looked at Elizabeth as he chewed, and nodded and smiled. She must be nearly forty now, like Dex. Thank God they were never foolish enough to marry, though no doubt Dexter had poked her when they were students. He felt like laughing. She was quite plainly not the marrying kind. Children out of the question. He saw her wide open eyes, her nervous nostrils, her desire to impress, something fancy and successful about her, and yet he felt sure she was the kind of woman who'd throw round terms like *the orthodox feminist position*. He washed down the crumbs with a swig of coffee and waited for her to speak. He guessed what she would say.

[6]

She did. 'Isn't Mrs Fox here?'

How sociable. He remembered her at nineteen. She made him an omelette for lunch when his wife was out, a clumsy act of duty, and called him to come and eat it, but he was upstairs nutting out a score and neither answered nor came till the food was cold and flat. She glowered at him from the scullery. The young women liked his wife more than they did him.

'No. My wife's at home. And that's where I'm going.'

His cultivated vowels: mai waife. She longed to whip the serviette out of his collar.

'Is that Dexter's little boy?'

Doctor Fox jumped. 'Yes. One of them. This is William.'

The child had vague eyes. Elizabeth, who was not good with small children, bent across the table and tried to get her face into his line of vision. The boy's gaze drifted, but not towards her. It was like looking at him through water. A smile of blessedness warmed his features and was gone; a little knot of thought bulged between his brows and smoothed itself again. She could not get his attention.

The old man cleared his throat. 'I'm afraid Billy's not quite . . .'

Elizabeth sat up.

'They didn't realise for quite a . . . He never spoke. He does sing. His voice is very . . . Dexter and his wife thought for a while he was some sort of musical genius. They can be toilet-trained, taught to keep themselves clean . . .'

Dexter came charging back. He had one arm above his head, holding a plate with cake on it. He plunged into the seat beside her. 'Shithouse cheese cake,' he roared. He reached across and wedged a piece of it into the little boy's mouth.

Doctor Fox would have got on the plane with the paper serviette still sprouting from his collar. Elizabeth whisked it out. He stood in front of her with his eyes closed like a child waiting to have its face wiped. She remembered a reference he had written for her when she went for her first job: 'an intellect of quite a high order'. Now it seemed comical, even a compliment; but then she had wept over the reservation. She screwed up the serviette and stepped back.

'I'll be forty soon,' she said.

Doctor Fox opened his eyes and let out a peculiar cry. 'Ah!

Then you will be out of the fog. At forty you can no longer harm anyone, and no-one can harm you.'

'What?' she thought. 'That can't possibly be true.' But it was exactly the kind of answer she had wanted.

He laughed and pulled a long face at her, then turned to kiss the child goodbye, but the boy's face was suffused with sudden bliss, and he flung open his arms as if the vision splendid had shimmered into view over his father's shoulder. Elizabeth too recoiled, as we do in respect and fear before the ecstasy of someone tripping on acid, to whom we are nothing more substantial than a liquid blur of light.

Elizabeth did not want to tell Dexter about her mother. Although the news was more than a year old, he would be so portentously and profoundly sorry for her that she would be embarrassed into making some smart crack, which would shock and grieve him and then he would rebuke her and she would not be able to prevent herself from blushing and hanging her head. She wanted to say, as well, 'Don't call me Morty. Nobody calls me that any more.' But that would sound snotty and he would laugh at her.

'Mum died,' she said. 'And don't you dare feel sorry for me.'

'She *died*.' He did not stop walking, or even turn his head to look at her. He had the weird boy slung over his shoulder like a saddle bag. He held out his arm to her. 'Take my arm, Morty,' he said. '*We'll go together down.* Who wrote that?'

'Browning. "My Last Duchess." '

'Dear Morty,' said Dexter.

'Also,' she said, 'I think I am about to get stuck with Vicki.'

He shook his head. He was still not looking at her. 'Morty. Morty. I know what it means to be stuck with someone. You mustn't think about it like that. It'll only make you miserable.'

They stopped at the gate lounge. The door opened.

'Here she comes,' said Elizabeth.

'Which one is she?' said Dexter.

The man walking behind Vicki was talking to his friend, he had a faint stammer, not much more than a hesitation. ''Mazing guy, Gaz. Always thinking about his mem, mem, member. There was something in his brain that just went sprong. He'd see a good looking chick dancing in front of the stage, he'd go down between sets and find her, and he'd be back five minutes later doing up his fly.'

His story was bodyless. A mosquito might have been whining it next to her ear. The footsteps of the hastening passengers beat light and fast. Either the windows were tinted or Melbourne was already dark.

The hostess at the open door showed her teeth. Vicki came out into the world. She saw the man beside Elizabeth and slowed down. That couldn't be Philip. Philip couldn't possibly look like that. Philip played in a *band*. She whipped off the rhinestone ear-rings and shoved them into her pocket.

The freeway was dark. Vicki's toes were so cold that they felt like rows of marbles inside her shoes. The strange boy was strapped into his car seat beside her. He mooed and murmured to himself. She stopped trying to listen to the conversation in the front, and stared out the window. Low down on the sky was a narrow band of apricot, all that was left of the daylight. Dexter threw back his head and laughed at something Elizabeth said. Vicki experienced the small prickle of power that comes to the one who rides in the back seat. She saw her captors as they would never see themselves: two silly heads of hair, two sets of shoulders, two unsuspecting napes. She hated them. She closed her eyes with hatred. Dexter saw her in the mirror and thought she had fallen asleep. Unresisted now, his tenderness for the whole world rushed to envelop her.

❖

Athena flung in broken briquettes and clanged the door shut. The pot-belly stove began to roar, then settled into its long single note. She spread out the *Herald* on the kitchen table. In the sports section there was a picture of a footballer with his baby. She hastened to turn the page. Now every baby photo

[9]

reminded her of the famous one of Azaria in its oval frame: the blurred form, pupa-like in swaddling, the wrinkled brow, the head turned sharply from the light, the fists and eyes squeezed shut. Athena kept her pointed scissors packed away, up high.

There was soup in the pot. 'Soup means lots!' Dexter would say when he came in. Where were they? She propped the Kabalevsky open on the piano and tried again. She had laboured through a dozen bars when the car slid down the driveway outside the kitchen window. More than two doors banged. She got up from the piano and took a knife to the rest of the loaf.

Dexter flooded in on a tide of cold air. He loved coming home.

'Athena! Look who's here!'

The three women stood still and stared at one another.

'Sisters,' thought Athena, with that start of wonder which family resemblance provokes. 'Big one's tough. Little one's miserable.'

'She's beautiful,' thought Vicki. 'It's warm. I wish I could live here.' Her chest loosened and she began to breathe.

'She's a frump,' thought Elizabeth with relief; but Athena stepped forward and held out her hand, and Elizabeth saw the cleverly mended sleeve of her jumper and was suddenly not so sure.

'Come in,' said Athena. 'Dexter, can't you close that door?'

Because it had only one source of light, a yellow-shaded standard lamp at head-height against a wall, the Fox family's kitchen was like a burrow, rounded rather than cubed, as if its corners had been stuffed with dry grass. The air shimmered with warmth. The table, large, wooden, scarred, was laid at one end with a bleached cotton cloth, a pile of bowls, a fistful of spoons. All the objects in the room looked like cartoons of themselves: the flap-handled fridge, the brown piano grinning, the dresser where plates leaned and cups hung.

Dexter made the presentations.

'We can't stay, I'm afraid,' said Elizabeth in her grand manner. The closed door next to the stove must lead to the bathroom: she could hear the dull splatter of a leaking shower tap.

'Yes you can,' said Dexter. He took the lid off the saucepan.

'Soup! Soup, Billy. Soup means lots. Sit up, everyone. Where's Arthur?'

'At the Papantuanos',' said Athena.

'I hope he's not watching TV.'

'They're making suits of armour in the shed.'

'I'll go and get him,' said Dexter. 'Athena – Vicki must be sat near the warmth. She's from sunnier climes, aren't you, Vicki.' He rounded her up, sidling and dancing with his arms out in their big curve. Vicki scowled with embarrassment, but obeyed. Elizabeth abandoned her plan to watch 'Sale of the Century', and allowed herself to be shuffled to a chair. She drew off her gloves.

A bigger boy ran in the back door, and kicked it to. He had the same home-cut hair as Billy's, a helmet of blond silk.

'Sit Billy up, Arthur,' said Dexter.

Arthur seized his brother by the shoulders and turned him towards the table where the others sat watching. 'Come on, Billy!' he shouted. He kept his eyes on his audience and made a great business of seating Billy on the bench. He stuck a spoon in the child's fist, and turned like an actor to face an ovation.

'What a ham,' thought Elizabeth.

'I wonder where their TV is,' thought Vicki.

Athena stood up with the ladle.

'Two four six eight, bog in don't wait,' said Dexter.

Vicki had never seen anything like Dexter at table. She was disgusted, and ashamed for him. He gripped the spoon so that the whole handle vanished in his paw; he bent over the bowl and slurped so loudly that he seemed not to be using the spoon at all, but to be transferring the food from bowl to mouth by suction alone. Athena could eat properly – why didn't she correct him in private? But Athena went on spooning up her soup, glancing from time to time at the children, and spread around her a shy, attentive calm which even Elizabeth, to whom Dexter's table manners were merely one more avenue to her complicated memories of his family, found soothing and agreeable.

Dexter emptied his bowl for the last time, then lifted it in both hands and licked it out, pushing his face right into it. There was soup on his nose, his chin and the front of his hair. He wiped it off on the sleeve of his jumper and sat back with a sigh. He was fed: now he could be sociable again. Nothing, thought Vicki, could be worse than the way he eats. Now things can only get better.

The soup was thick. The bread was fresh. The stove's dry heat reddened their cheeks. The walls curved in around them. Outside the house, which was at the bottom of a neglected street, no cars passed.

Not late, but in a starry cold that lifted them off their feet, they went out to the car.

'Christ, it's cold,' said Elizabeth.

'But you can smell things growing,' said Dexter. 'Not long now.'

'Still the mindless optimist.'

'Where's the toilet?' said Vicki.

'Right down in the corner of the yard,' said Dexter.

Vicki lit the candle. The door would not stay shut. She had to keep one knee against it so that the sound of her meek trickling would not escape into the black air. She wiped herself. The door swung open. Just as she reached up for the chain, she heard a noise. Something trotted, something dragged itself. She stood still with her hand hooked through the metal loop. The noise came again, a small and intimate sound. She blew out the candle and sight returned like the slow relaxing of a muscle. Ten feet out from the lavatory door was a cage, a derelict chook pen, covered in creeper. Something in the cage was shifting in its straw.

Up there under the leafless vine they were talking. Vicki saw their breath. From the angles of their bodies she could tell they were arguing. Dexter was trying to make Elizabeth do something.

'It's not my job,' she said. 'Why the hell should I?'

'Because no-one else will,' said Dexter. 'Because there's nothing else. What else *is* there? Otherwise we're all just dry leaves blowing down the gutter.'

Vicki got into the car and kept her face against the side window. She saw sour street lights, a house standing in a junk yard: old washing machines, tea-chests, a car with no wheels. Elizabeth sat silent with folded arms. Dexter sang aloud in a foreign language.

They turned into a long, important-looking street with silver

[12]

tramlines. The buildings looked like closed shops. They had flat fronts and stone vases on their roofs.

'This is it, Dexter. Stop here.'

Elizabeth got out and slammed the door. She looked up and down the street with her hands in her pockets. Vicki dragged her suitcase on to the pavement. Dexter did not want to abandon her. He blundered out of the car and skipped behind the two silent women to the door of the building.

'Vicki! You must come to our place whenever you like! Athena's always there. Come round the back. We never lock the door.'

She turned her bleached face to him and gave a small nod. Elizabeth rammed the key into the lock and twisted it back and forth. Dexter looked at the shopfronts opposite. One of them had a dull red light over the door; its number was painted in numerals as tall as a man.

'Morty!' he said. 'Shouldn't you be living in a proper house?'

'Oh shutup. You're worse than Mum.'

Dexter fell back to the edge of the pavement and they went past him into the building. The street door clashed behind them.

Elizabeth took the stairs very fast, making a lot of heel noise. Her coat billowed and Vicki tramped in a wave of perfume. They went up and up. The staircase was concrete. At the very top there was another big door.

Elizabeth strode straight across the boards to the bed and pulled a cassette player out from behind it. She shoved in a tape and went to the bare window; she turned her back on Vicki and stood with her feet apart and her hands on her hips. She looks like a record cover, thought Vicki. Tape hissed, music burst out. Elizabeth begin to dance: no, not to dance, but to move her body, to sway forward from the waist, as if she were on a stage, as if the audience were outside the black window.

What is this, thought Vicki. What is in here? It is a warehouse, it has no walls or rooms. There is a row of windows, each one shaped like an eye with its brow raised. There is a TV, a phone on the floor, a bed like a big pink cloud. Where does she cook? Where does she wash herself? Where will *I* sleep? Everybody needs a bed. There are no walls or rooms.

Elizabeth turned round and saw her standing there beside her suitcase. She was ashamed. She turned down the music.

'I'm not set up,' she said. 'Tonight you'd better sleep with me. Tomorrow we'll think about what to do.'

The sisters got into the bed: it was cold and there was no sofa and nothing else to do. Elizabeth sat up and crocheted. Vicki lay flat, and kept well out to one side so as not to be in the way. She thought, 'I'll be awake all night. I must try to keep still.' The tops of her thighs went numb. But she did doze, swam lightly away under the quilt, under three inches of sunny water, crows flapped against the wind high up near the blades of the windmill, all her papers blew away, her nerves gave a jolt and she woke with her heart thumping.

'Look, Vicki. It's the Pope.'

Vicki sat up. On the bright little screen at the foot of the bed a man in a white skullcap moved slowly along a row of people. He stretched out his hands in a quiet, formal manner, he smiled and inclined his head, he leaned to them. Someone held up a child and out came his hands, fingers spread starwise like a blind man's, to touch the baby's cheeks and temples. His movements were so exaggeratedly slow, and from this slowness emanated such theatrical power, that he reminded Vicki of a spaceman.

'He's weightless,' she said.

'You were asleep.'

'What's he doing?'

'Blessing them, I suppose. What a lot of mumbo jumbo.'

'Don't you think blessing does any good?'

Elizabeth looked up sharply, as one does at a small child who asks its first coherent question. 'No. No, I don't, actually.'

'It looks nice though. Don't you think? I wish someone would bless me.'

Elizabeth twitched her crochet hook in and out. A sucker for a cult, she thought. Better keep her out of the city at night. 'The last time anybody blessed me,' she said, 'was when I took a bag of old clothes to the Salvation Army opshop. But I did get myself baptised when I was a student.'

'Did they push you right under?'

'I wasn't a fundamentalist, thanks very much. Just a cross on the forehead, a bit of nice music, turn to the east, forswear the devil and all his works. And guess who my godfather was. Dexter.'

'But he's the same age as you.'

'I know.'

'What would he know about it?'

'You don't have to know anything. Just turn up on the day.'

'That's terrible,' said Vicki. 'That's really terrible. I think things like that ought to be stricter, if people are going to do them at all. Otherwise they don't make sense.'

❖

'You have to tell me a story,' said Poppy to her father. 'Before you go to work.'

'You're too old,' said Philip. 'Why don't you just read, or do some practice?'

'It's not the same. It's no fun on my own.'

'Don't make me feel guilty,' he said. 'Someone has to bring home the bacon.'

'Why can't you work in the daytime like everybody else?'

'I can't, and you know why. I don't know any stories any more.'

'Yes you do. Stories from your life. Just make something up, like you used to. It's easy. You go 'Once upon a time', and then say whatever comes into your head.'

She plumped up the doona and moved over to make room for him. He sat down on the edge of the bed. 'When you go to high school next year,' he said, 'are you going to tell your friends your father still tells you a story every night?'

'That depends,' said Poppy, 'on whether they're the right sort of person. Come on. I'm listening.'

'Once upon a time,' said Philip. 'There was a wonderful cafe. It opened very early in the morning. No. It stayed open twenty-four hours. It never closed. They never turned off the machine. That's why the coffee was perfect.'

It was easy. He slid into it.

'At night, because of the noise of people laughing, they turned up the treble on the jukebox. But in the early mornings, in the peaceful shift when customers on their way to work were reading the papers, you could clearly hear the trip and run of the bass lines. Some people came alone, with a library book, dressed in clean clothes of sober cut and colour. Others brought their children and taught them, with smiles and soft words, how to behave in a public place. The clever children read aloud to their parents from the Situations Vacant, the Houses to Let. The big windows of the cafe faced east. People sat with their backs to the sun, and the iron bars of night softened in their shoulders. On the other side of the road, which sparkled with passing cars, a deep garden overflowed its iron fence.'

He glanced at her to see if he was getting too fanciful. She was looking at the ceiling. 'Don't drone,' she said, 'You're starting to drone.'

'It was a place that waited,' said Philip. 'It was a place of reason and courtesy. On the jukebox they had Elvis Presley. They had Elisabeth Schwarzkopf. They had Les Paul and Mary Ford singing "How High the Moon".

'People danced there, in the daytime, in the middle of the morning, down the aisle between the two long rows of tables. The songs they favoured were South American ones with titles the Australians passed over in ignorance, thinking them Italian: the songs were more passionate, more driven, more intellectual than anything we know of here. They danced in each other's arms, with their elbows up high and no expression on their faces: it was all form and precision. They did the tango, the rhumba, the samba. They knew the steps. They never stumbled. Their arms and legs were long and sinewy. The dresses were a spray of light. The men's trousers hit the shoe just right.

'There were two waiters. Neither of them had ever forgotten an order in his life. Kon, a Greek, was as handsome as a statue, cheerful and young. He had a glossy folder of photos of himself and wanted to get into modelling. Marcello was a reformed gambler with slicked-back hair and an expression of weary, courtly bitterness. He stood behind the machine, he held a drawer open with his thigh and counted money. He had confidence with a wad. He pinched each note between thumb and forefinger. He had been in Australia twenty years but he could still hardly speak English.

'There was graffiti in the lavatories. Linda Lovelace's mother went down on the Titanic. Lisa is a slut. Renato is a spunk and you molls will never have him signed Lucy and Maria. People in the Paradise Bar read the daily graffiti as if it was the news of the world.'

'As if it were,' said Poppy.

'The Paradise Bar does not serve alcohol. It doesn't need to. Something happens, once you pass that heavy fly curtain . . . Are you listening?'

It was dark. The television was turned down low in the other room. Poppy was dropping off. She rallied.

'Yes. Keep going. Once you passed the . . . '

'The Gaggia hissed. Behind it on a shelf stood a row of triangular bottles, red and green and yellow.'

He paused. She was breathing steadily.

'Pop?'

No answer. He dropped his voice and began to speak more rapidly. 'At night it's different. The waiters are low-browed and covered in tattoos. They wear black jeans and tight T-shirts. They look more like crims or bouncers than waiters. When they set down a cup of coffee some of it slops into the saucer. The owner of the Paradise Bar seems uncertainly in control of his employees. Dope is bought and sold at the Paradise Bar. It is not the kind of place outside which you would like to see your daughter sitting, under the Cinzano umbrellas. On Saturday nights you cannot get a seat at any of its twenty tables. The marbled concrete floor is slippery with spilt liquid. Occasionally some girl, limp with excess, collapses into the arms of her shrieking friends. They hustle her outside, holding her by the shoulders and the ribcage. Her feet in their flat shoes drag behind her in ballet position. Hot Valiants cruise close to the kerb, gunning their motors. The games jingle their piercing tunes in the big back room, the air is thick with smoke, other things are going on upstairs. The Italian kids walk in and out with a lot of money on their backs. They walk in and out, shaking out their expensive haircuts, shaking

[17]

their glossy Italian hair.'

She was fast asleep. He did not know whether she had done her homework. For dinner they had gulped a souvlaki, walking home through the park. He got off the bed. At the door he turned round and said in a whisper,

'And men fuck girls without loving them. Girls cry in the lavatories. Work, Poppy. Use your brains.'

Maybe Elizabeth would come over. He left the car keys on the table just in case.

That night at the studio they finished early. There were no taxis, so he walked. He didn't know what time it was but thought it must be after two. The cafe was still open, hollow as a Hopper painting behind the empty bus shelter. Philip passed on the other side of the street, too far away to determine the sex of a couple of white-faced students who were sitting at a corner table under the neon sign, not talking to each other. He plugged on up the rise towards the housing commission flats. By the time he passed the first block he was singing to himself, some old Stevie Winwood song with a riff that made him think of that small figure, arms outspread, hovering like a mosquito between banks of keyboards.

There were people against the railings of the carpark. Six, or eight. His skin stood up. It was dark. He made air go in, and out, and kept walking. They stood quietly and let him pass. He waited for the thump in the back, in the neck, the foot stuck out to trip. He wanted something to happen, left right left right come *on*.

'Hey, you.'

He propped and spun round. The briefcase swung out from his side.

'What's in that bag.'

He felt his charming smile push up the flesh of his cheeks, the vertical wrinkles form beside his mouth. He took a step towards the boy he thought had spoken, lowered his head and nodded many times.

'Money,' he said in a conversational tone. 'Money, and drugs.'

The boy was too young: he looked quickly left and right. Was it a joke? He had no answer. He twisted his face away in a grimace of disgust and self-consciousness, as if a teacher had ticked him off, and fell back among the other children against the rail.

Was that all?

❖

Vicki woke. Elizabeth was still sleeping, with her face to the wall. Her hair, flattened in the night, had formed matted curls which reminded Vicki against her will of what can be seen inside vacuum cleaners or the ripped seat of railway carriages. From the street downstairs, out the raised-eyebrow windows, rose a screeching of metal. Vicki slid out from under the pink quilt and went to the window, but the tram had launched itself again and was away, its little flag fluttering. The room was so high above the street that there was no need for curtains.

Vicki poked around and found a partition behind which there was a bath with one of those hand squirter things she had only ever seen in magazines. She squatted down and washed herself carefully. There was a lot of steam and when she pushed open the fire-escape door beside the bath a gumtree branch presented itself right in front of her. She leaned out and put her face among the leaves: their edges were as hard as school rulers, the air was cold. She could see a fire escape of wooden stairs and tubular railings, and a narrow yard out of which the tree came soaring straight up as if fighting the building for space. A woman in a blue coat hurried across the carpark with a fat satchel in her arms.

In the huge room beyond the partition the phone rang and she heard Elizabeth pick it up. Before the caller had a chance to speak, Elizabeth said in a slow, low, very distinct voice, 'Don't *ever* ring this number at this hour, ever again. Is that clear?' Vicki turned off the taps and stood in the bath. Sensible plans

[19]

of action such as 'Step out on to the floor' or 'Call out and ask her for a towel' clicked their wooden sides together without meaning, like building blocks. She heard bed-clothes rustle, then a stillness. If she stood there long enough the drops of water would dry on her. Would her whole life be made up of these moments? The difference between these moments and being dead was that live people were always supposed to be doing something. Dead people could just shrivel. Her mother was lying on her back in a dark box, crabbed and cramped as a bat; her arms and legs were drawn up against her torso by the hourly drying and tightening of her skin which was by now no longer skin but had become cracked leather, dark reddish brown and ridged and shiny like what you saw on cooked ducks in Chinese food shops. Vicki had an idea that this was not scientifically accurate but she preferred this theory to thinking about dampness and worms. She closed the fire escape door as quietly as she could. There was no sound from the bed.

❖

Vicki ran her hand along the rack of pink and green T-shirts. The radio was on in the shop. Music stopped and a man read the news. 'A twelve-year-old girl, shipwrecked three years ago and given up for dead, has been found alive in the jungle of Sumatra, covered in moss. It is believed that she kept herself alive by absorbing pollen through her skin.'

Two salesgirls were leaning against the front counter. One of them was holding a bottle of metho and a soft cloth. Their eyes met.

'Moss?' said one. 'Pfff. She absorbed *pollen* through her *skin?*'

They laughed. Vicki watched them closely, ready to be included in their amusement, to roll her shoulders in scepticism as they did, but they pretended not to see her and turned back to their contemplation of the street outside. In a minute one of them would come over and tell Vicki to stop handling the clothes.

Vicki knew what her retort would be: 'Don't be *silly*.' She would turn her mouth down, and her eyes would become cold, glittering slits. And if a waiter said anything to her about going straight through to the toilet without being a customer of the cafe, she would put her hand on her hip and say, 'First I piss, then I eat – do you *mind*?' And then she would order something *really cheap*, like one donut or a packet of CCs. In this frame of mind, savage with homesickness and loneliness, she roamed the city, daring it to tackle her. It paid her no attention.

Athena understood why people gave up playing an instrument. She knew she did not play well, that her playing, even when correct, was like someone reciting a lesson in an obedient voice, without inflection or emotion, without understanding: a betrayal of music. She took her hands off the keyboard. There was dust on all the keys except those an octave either side of middle C. She closed the lid.

She stood at the tramstop opposite the long railed side of the cemetery. Someone had written in black texta on the lamp-post DARREN WAR LOURD. No tram was in sight, but she saw an orange campervan coming fast down the street, heading south. It had neat curtains and a sink, and a lone man at the wheel. He and Athena exchanged a friendly look and she got in and he turned the van round and drove the other way, on to the freeway and out past the turn-off to the airport and the Italian houses with white porticos and palm trees, past the city limits and the wreckers' yards and the paddocks where broken-winded horses stood patiently at the wire and out on to the great basalt plains with their tall thistles nodding, and further and further until it was desert with a sky so dry and high that they slept out on the ground at night with never a drop of dew.

There was still no tram coming. It was lazy to wait when she could be walking, and only three-quarters of a mile.

When Vicki saw her for the second time, Athena was standing in the wide doorway of the bookshop, arms folded and head tilted back, scanning the window covered in hand-printed cards on which people advertised rooms to let in their rented houses. Athena lived, for as long it took to read a card, in each sunny cottage, attractive older-style flat, spacious house, quaint old terrace, large balcony room with fireplace, collective household with thriving veggie garden. Her children dematerialised, her husband died painlessly in a fall from a mountain. What curtains she would sew! What private order she would establish and maintain, what handfuls of flowers she would stick in vegemite jars, how sweetly and deeply she would sleep, and between what fresh sheets!

Vicki saw Athena's foot in its thick sock and sandal. She wanted Athena to recognise her, but she prepared a speech of reminder just in case, though it galled her that all she could think of to say was 'Remember me? I'm Morty's sister.' She reached out and tugged at Athena's sleeve. Athena jumped and turned and blushed. She's *shy*, thought Vicki.

'Vicki! Are you all right?' The girl was white, and looked tightly bound into her clothes.

Vicki nodded. Until that moment she had not realised that she was not all right. 'I feel a bit funny,' she said. 'I feel as if part of my brain has sort of come away, at the back.' She raised one hand to indicate the trouble spot.

A hypochondriac, thought Athena. 'Is Elizabeth here too?'

'No. She's still asleep. I can't live there. There's only one bed. I was looking at the house ads.'

'Does Elizabeth know?'

'Know what?'

'She'll want you to stay with her, won't she?'

Vicki began to jabber. 'Do you want to know what kind of person Elizabeth is? She's the kind of person who doesn't slow down when she comes to an automatic door. She buys herself a pair of jeans and gives them to you straight away because they're stiff and she's too impatient to wear them in, then three months later when they're all broken in and perfect, she asks for them back.'

[22]

Embarrassed, they looked away at the window full of white cards.

'There are some nice-sounding places,' said Athena. The girl was in a state.

'Yes, except this one,' said Vicki. She crouched down and pointed to a grubby notice right at the bottom of the mass. Athena bent over. 'To let,' it said. 'One room, limited daylight only, $25 per week. NB house *not* communal.'

'Limited daylight!' Vicki let out a pant of laughter. As Elizabeth had done when Vicki gave her opinion of papal benediction, Athena looked at the girl with sharpened attention.

'What are you going to do now?' said Vicki. 'I haven't got anything to do.'

They went into a cafe and sat at a table. Music was playing, not the usual kind of music you hear on a jukebox. The back door of the cafe had been left open; through it they saw new leaves, a lane. An Italian man with a narrow, tired face and a stern parting served them.

'What will you do, in Melbourne?' said Athena. 'You'll go back to school, won't you?'

Vicki shrugged. 'On the plane,' she said, 'I read a tourist book. I want to go and look at old monuments.'

'You mean – like the Shrine?'

'No. Old houses. Famous ones with all the furniture in them, and you can see how the servants did the cooking, and the funny bathrooms. Elizabeth hates that kind of thing.'

'I can't believe she's really as bad as all that,' said Athena.

The coffee came.

'What's that in the cage in your yard, Athena?'

'A rabbit. I'm going to let it out.'

'Won't cats eat it?'

'Not if I take it to the country.'

'Once humans have touched them,' said Vicki, 'the other animals can smell it on them, and they kill them. Nature red in tooth and claw.' She curved her fingers and bared her teeth.

Again Athena stared at her. There was a sudden flutter of colour in the corner of her eye. 'What was that?'

'I saw it too,' said Vicki. 'I think there's a lady out the back with a net dress on.'

'At eleven o'clock in the morning?'

'Maybe she's getting married.' Vicki blew on her coffee. 'Funny music, isn't it. Arab or something.'

'It's a tango', said Athena.

✜

Spring came. In the mornings, when the first person opened the back door, the whole bulk of air in the house shifted and warmed. Women sighed in expensive dress shops, as if even to contemplate fine stuffs were too much to bear. Dexter took Arthur to the National Gallery. On the way he spoke to the boy in magisterial tones about the lives of artists: Dexter loved tales of exalted suffering, of war and failure and unsympathetic wives and alcoholism. Arthur loitered in front of an etching called *Se Repulen*: two devils, one wielding a huge pair of scissors with which he was about to cut the other's toenails. 'Looks like me and Mum,' said Arthur.

Philip, too, got out the clippers and trimmed Poppy's toe-nails while she recited, for her exam, the circulation of the blood. 'The right atrium contracts,' she droned, 'and the left . . . ' 'I thought it was "auricle",' said Philip. 'It used to be,' said Poppy, 'but not any more. They've changed the name.' 'How the hell can they change the name of something?' said Philip. He dug the lower blade of the clippers under the nail of her big toe and snapped the handle to. She gasped. The lump of nail flew across the room and bounced off the desk leg.

Elizabeth used the presence of Vicki at her place as an excuse for sleeping nearly every night at Philip's. He did not mind: he was not the kind of person who could be bothered minding. But he stayed out later, fell into strange beds in houses where a boiling saucepan might as easily contain a syringe as an egg; he excited pointless passions in girls who knew no better than to sprawl for hours among empty pizza boxes at the studio and wait for somebody to notice them. He came home at that hour when light is not yet anything more than the exaggerated whiteness of a shirt flung against a bookcase, a higher gloss on the back of a kitchen chair. Poppy left her writings on the table and he read them eagerly: her happy flights of fancy, her visions of an adult world, her lists of invented names: the endless ingenuity of the only child. 'Finn and Angela have arrived on Dasnin,' he read in the light of the open refrigerator, 'to find an abandoned and desertous planet completely devoid of any living form.' If he came home late enough he found her sitting up to her solitary breakfast. She had cleared the table and placed before her a cup of tea and a plate of toast and bacon. She had already been out for a jog around the park. She was clean and bright. She read as she ate; some great work or other, *Norah of Billabong, The Once and Future King*. She did not leap up and swamp him with greetings: she raised her face to him with her composed, modest smile. All about her was the order which she had created. God, the joy of her, the pleasure! He put down his guitar case. Will anyone ever love her as much as he does?

Vicki slept and woke alone in the high room. She was scrupulous about keeping her clothes in the suitcase, out of the way behind the partition. One day she tried on all her sister's things: the slender shoes, the Italian cotton, the crushable linen, garments whose subtle cut invested their mannish shapes with a femininity so intense that Vicki, standing before the mirror, saw herself to be not yet an adult sexual being. She staggered to the fire escape in the towering heels, pushed open the door, and walked straight into the tree. Its fingery leaves flicked her across the open eye and she cried out and crouched with her hands over her face, blinded with shock and gushes of chemical tears. A voice she did not recognise as her own choked and groaned. She crawled back inside in the stupid shoes and curled up on the bed, weeping with self-pity and foolishness. She wanted to tell Athena.

The back door was open. She tiptoed down the passage. Athena was lying under a blanket on the big bed with her back to the door.

'Are you sick?' said Vicki.

'No,' said Athena. 'Just having a read before the kids get home.'

'Don't get up,' said Vicki. 'I'll sit at the desk and draw or something.'

The scratching of the lead pencil put Athena to sleep. She half-woke once or twice, when the phone rang and Vicki scampered down the hall to answer it, and when music came floating from the kitchen radio and plates rattled dully in water. Good grief, thought Athena, she's washing up.

Athena's life was mysterious to Vicki. She seemed contained, without needs, never restless.

'I'm bored,' said Vicki. 'Un-bore me, Thena!'

Athena laughed. 'I don't even know what boredom is.'

But how could she not know? thought Vicki, watching jealously out the front window the arrival of Athena's friend to visit with her two children: the slow ritual of getting out of the car, the back door held open against the hip, the unstrapping of small bodies, the unloading of the blue plastic nappy bag, the toys, the pencils, the Viking helmet, the Maya temple colouring book; the endless patience with the whining, twining children; the slow talking about nothing in particular; the friend gasbagging about health and sickness while Athena stood ironing at the board, keeping her head half-turned to show that she was still listening.

'The woman next door,' said the friend, 'went and had colonic irrigations. And the lady who did them found stuff inside her that she'd eaten *ten years* ago!'

'How could she tell?' said Athena.

'*Anyway*,' said the friend, 'she rang up and told me he'd gone off with some *child*, a girl of eighteen. So I said to her, "Get some interesting knitting. Something with a complicated pattern. And stay home and just *sit it out*." And that's what she did.'

They were talking like this when Vicki left to have her hair cut, and they were still talking like this when she got back, the only difference being that the table was now covered in dirty cups and cake crumbs.

'Look!' cried Vicki. 'Now I feel *terrific*. Is that red mark on the back of my neck still there? Do you know what that is? She cut the squared-off bit at the back with those shears.'

'Clippers?' said the friend.

'Yes! Clippety clip! And once she was going clippety clip right into my skin!' She gave a high, excited laugh.

The two mothers looked at her with their calm smiles. She felt as jerky as a puppet.

'Last time I had my hair cut short back home,' Vicki chattered on, rushing to the round mirror in the corner, 'I looked so ugly that I cried all night. And when I woke up in the morning my eyes were so swollen that I looked like a *cane* toad!'

'You certainly don't look ugly now,' said the friend, in her slow drawl.

'I know!' said Vicki. 'I'm so elegant now that I ought to be lined up and *shot*!'

The friend laughed, but Athena heard Vicki trying for Elizabeth's smart tone, and it squeezed her heart.

Vicki began to hang round the Foxes' house in Bunker Street earlier each day. They heard her old pushbike crash against the rubbish bins at breakfast time. She sprang up the concrete steps, checked her hair in the glass, and stayed an hour; ate an egg that Dexter had poached for himself; tried to make herself useful and agreeable, though she was domestically incompetent: she tipped tea-leaves down the sink and blocked it; she put embers from the pot-belly stove into a plastic bucket and melted it. But she began to know where things were, she was cheerful company, she laughed at Dexter's jokes, she played with Arthur. She laced his boots for him, though he had been able to do it himself for years.

'Can I walk down to school with you?' she said. 'Do you mind?'

'Yes,' said Arthur, with his nose in a cereal packet.

'You do mind?'

'I mean yes, you can come.'

When the mail arrived and Athena opened envelopes, Vicki watched and said, 'I never get any letters.'

Athena suppressed an impulse to say, 'You can read mine.'

Vicki loved their lavatory in the corner of the yard, its shelves made of brick and timber stuffed with old paperbacks, broken tools, camping gear and boxes of worn-down coloured pencils. She loved the notes they left for each other, the drawings and silly rhymes, the embarrassing singing, the vegetable garden, the fluster under which lay a generous order, the rushes of activity followed by periods of sunny calm: Vicki was in love with the house, with the family, with the whole establishment of it.

'Bunker Street is her *god*,' said Elizabeth.

Dexter was flattered. 'I feel sentimental when I see you, Morty,' he said. 'Why don't you bring this Philip round here?'

'Philip? What would I bring him here for?'

'He's your bloke, isn't he? Aren't you going to get married one of these days?'

Elizabeth shouted with laughter. 'Marry *him*? Forget it! He's already married! And anyway can you see me as a married woman?'

Dexter clenched his fists and danced up and down on the spot. 'But I *want* you to be happily married!'

Elizabeth raised her eyes to the ceiling.

'I don't understand the way you live,' said Dexter. 'What are the rules? Does he – you know – betray you?'

'Of course he bloody "betrays" me,' said Elizabeth. 'When you've been with someone that long, what else is there to do?'

Dexter flung out his arms and turned to Vicki who was at the mirror by the piano trying to tie a scarf round her head.

'I hate modern life,' he said. 'Modern American manners.'

'It's just love,' said Vicki, turning and twisting to get a back view of herself.

'Love!' roared Dexter. 'I've never been in love, then. In *lerve*. I don't even know what it is. What's so funny?'

'You'll find out one day,' said Elizabeth.

'I don't see why people think falling *in lerve* is inevitable,' said Dexter. 'Anyone would think it was some kind of disease, or plague. People only fall in lerve because they've read about it in some cheap American magazine, because they *want* to, because they're bored and have nothing better to do. I don't want to, therefore I'm not going to.'

'But weren't you in love with Athena?' said Vicki, scandalised.

'No,' said Dexter. 'Not in that tortured way you read about.'

Vicki looked quickly at Athena, afraid she would be hurt, but

Athena was smiling and listening.

'You're not really a scarf person, are you, Vicki,' said Elizabeth.

Vicki yanked the scarf off her head.

'Who's the pianist round here?' said Elizabeth. She flipped up the lid and struck a note or two.

'Athena plays, don't you dear,' said Dexter.

'Well, I'm learning,' said Athena. She was keeping her back to the room.

'How about playing us something?' said Elizabeth.

'Oh no – I'm hopeless.'

'Come on. No false modesty.'

'No, really!' said Athena. She turned from the sink with the knife in her hand. 'You don't realise what an elementary stage I'm at.'

'You can't be that bad,' said Elizabeth. She opened the book. *The Children's Bach.* God, listen to this – how pompous. "Bach is never simple, but that is one reason why we should all try to master him." Show us how you've mastered him, Athena!'

'Oh, please don't make me,' said Athena. 'Please. I can hardly play at all.'

'It's true,' said Vicki. 'She can't. You play like a mouse. I heard you plinking away in here the other day and I thought, poor Thena!'

Athena turned back to the sink.

'Yes, dear,' said Dexter. 'You ought to practise when you're the only one home.' He turned over a page of the newspaper. 'It's a bit dreary having to listen to someone picking their way through those pieces.'

He sat reading at the table with Billy on his knee. Vicki folded the scarf. Athena shifted the potatoes about under the dribbling tap.

Elizabeth braced herself. 'Vicki wouldn't remember this,' she said, 'but our mother had a saying. She told it to me when I realised my voice wasn't going to be quite as fabulous as I'd hoped. *If only those birds sang that sang the best, how silent the woods would be.*'

'Clumsy syntax,' said Dexter. '*Woods* and *would* right next to each other.'

'Say it again?' said Athena.

[29]

'If only those birds sang – that sang the best – how silent the woods would be.'

'She must have been a nice woman,' said Athena.

'I don't know if nice is quite the word,' said Elizabeth. 'She was the sort of person who'd put on Ravel's *Bolero* first thing in the morning. And she had a voice like somebody falling off a mountain.'

'Shutup, Elizabeth,' said Vicki. 'She *was* nice! She was! Just because *you* didn't –'

'She used to like ironing,' said Elizabeth. 'The easy stuff – you know, tablecloths, hankies. She got cancer.'

'I know,' said Athena. 'Vicki told me.'

'She wouldn't go into hospital,' said Vicki.

'That must have made things hard for you,' said Athena. What selfishness, she thought. *I* would have been more sensible. 'Why on earth wouldn't she go?'

'Well,' said Elizabeth, 'I suppose that would have been admitting to herself that she was going to die.'

It was a patient and courteous answer to an ignorant question. Athena felt ground drop away from under her feet. She hung over a black gulf, she heard the wind. Her self was in tantrum, panicking. *What? Me* die? Life go on without *me*? Impossible! It was briefer than a pulse. It was over before she had time to gasp. She held the hard potato in her hand. For the first time she looked at Elizabeth properly, with open face.

Billy drew a breath and started to scream in short, sharp cries. He flung himself back on Dexter's lap; he clapped his left hand over his ear, and bit into the heel of his right hand, held it against his large crooked teeth and pressed, pressed. He went 'Eeeeee!' high up in his skull.

'Quiet, Billy,' said Dexter in a firm, pleasant voice. 'Shhh. No more screams.'

He stopped at once, but moaned and would have gone on biting himself had Dexter not drawn his hands away and held them. Two streets away a tram chattered. The wail of an ambulance faded in spasms.

'What's the matter with him?' whispered Vicki. 'Why is he biting himself?'

'It's the sirens,' said Dexter. 'They drive him crazy. Sometimes they're so far away that we can't even hear them. He's like a dog.'

The boy became calm. Athena dropped the cleaned potatoes into a colander.

Vicki too could brace herself. She said, 'Would he come for a walk with me?' Dexter and Athena turned to look at her. They are astonished, thought Elizabeth.

'Are you sure?' said Dexter. 'Most people –'

Vicki blossomed in their surprise, smug as a child whose mother has commended her for doing a small piece of house-work without having to be asked.

Dexter slid Billy off his lap and she gripped his hand. It was warm and padded with muscle. She spoke to him and he smiled past her.

'Why won't he ever look at me?'

'Don't bother to get romantic,' said Athena. 'There's nobody *in* there.'

She watched them go down the back steps hand in hand, and from the kitchen table Elizabeth watched Athena and waited for her to turn around and show the expression on her face, which, when she did, was not quite what Elizabeth had imagined.

'How do you bear it?' she said.

'Bear it?' Was this one of Elizabeth's dramatic exclamations, or did she really want to know? 'I've abandoned him, in my heart,' said Athena. 'It's work. I'm just hanging on till we can get rid of him.'

'Get *rid* of him?' said Elizabeth.

Athena's small, calm smile did not alter. 'The thought of it,' she said in her civilised voice, 'the very thought of it is like a dark cloud rolling away.'

'There might be a place for him, in a year or so,' said Dexter. He stood up and stretched his limbs. 'You know, sometimes he screams all day.'

'Dex is still romantic about him,' said Athena.

The women looked at Dexter. He shrugged.

'*I* used to be romantic about him,' said Athena. 'I used to think there was some kind of wild, good little creature trapped inside him, and I tried to communicate with that. But now I know there's . . .' (she knocked her forehead with her knuckles) '. . . nobody home.'

'And what about you, Morty,' said Dexter. 'What are you going to do about your sister?'

Vicki and the boy crossed the street and stepped on to the buffalo grass. It was early evening. The trunks were grey, the leaves were green, a mild wind was moving along. Bigger boys were swooping about under the trees on elongated bicycles. Fuck off, cunt! Dickhead! Their words to each other were blows, their laughter rattled like guns. Vicki spoke to Billy as one speaks to an animal or a baby, murmuring encouragement without expecting an answer. She tried to walk him neatly along the bitumen path, but he was unruly, he grunted and tugged at her hand. He dragged her across the grass to the swings. She heaved him on to the metal seat, clamped his fists round the chains and began to push him from behind.

She pushed so hard that his backward oscillation, had she wedged her fingertips between his hard bum and the seat, would have lifted her right off the ground. When she heard his voice she thought he was going to start screaming again, but it was a song. She pushed and pushed, until at the top of each forward flight he lay on his back in air. What was that song? Of course he sang no words, only a round-mouthed ooh-oohing, but the tune was perfect, its rhythm was timed to the rushes and pauses of the swing, and his voice was high, sweet and melodious. She let the metal seat raise her, she hooked her fingers over its edge, sent him flying away from her and threw up her arms to receive him again. He sang a verse, a chorus, another verse, and the words ran back to her in her mother's voice and she joined in: 'Speed, bonny boat, like a bird on the wing/Onward! the sailors cry.'

The foul boys on bikes fled away down the darkening avenues of trees, a light flicked on outside the public lavatory, and still she pushed and sang. He could not get enough. She ran round in front of the swing to look at his face: it was a pink blur, he was in ecstasy. She was bored. She tried to change the song, but he let out such a scream that she bit it off in mid-phrase. They probably didn't even have a radio, or if they did it was permanently stuck on the ABC. She slackened the force of her pushing and he writhed on the seat and clanked the chains. His rhythm left him and he hung close to the ground, dangling and roaring. He would not look at her, he would not get off. She made him, and dragged him away across the grass. They turned a corner, rounded a thick hedge, and the wind hit them. He stopped struggling. Air rushed over the ground like a flood of water at blood temperature, and he pulled himself free of her and went into it pacing slowly like a dancer, his arms spread out and his face tipped back, his eyes closed and his mouth melting.

He made her sick. He was empty, open, nothing but a conduit for meaningless rage or bliss. She wrenched at him, pulled him towards home, but he trailed, he tugged, he smiled weakly into the warm air. She let go his hand again and he drifted towards the edge of the footpath. In the half-dark a heavy truck blundered round the corner. The ground shuddered under her foot-soles, it tickled her, and in a rapture of disgust she saw Billy step off the pavement into the gutter. Quick, better for everyone. She took two long steps, she gave him a light shove between the shoulder blades, and he walked out under it. The huge wheels swallowed him up like a bunch of beans in a blender and he was gone, not even a stain on the bitumen.

Athena was in the kitchen and the light was on.

'There was a big truck,' said Vicki. 'And I thought, I could push him under it. Do you ever, have you ever –'

'Of course,' said Athena. 'Hundreds of times.'

She took hold of the boy by the shoulders and turned him towards the bathroom. He submitted with glazed eyes and a drunken smile. As he passed Vicki he leaned on her and rubbed his back against her hip. His buttocks rested against her thigh and she felt the warmth and depth of his flesh.

So Vicki came to live with the Fox family at Bunker Street. They moved the junk out of the small room behind the kitchen; it overlooked the vegetable garden and the shed and the rabbit's cage and the Hills Hoist and the European trees, thick with new leaves, that grew along the banks of the Merri

Creek. Athena and Vicki painted the room yellow. 'I'll be like a chicken in an egg,' said Vicki. Elizabeth thought the yellow was rather ochreous, but in her relief she kept this opinion to herself. She went home on the tram and was surprised to find a small lack in herself, a blankness where the unwelcome responsibility had been. She flung the pink quilt out to air over the windowsill and went into the city to buy herself a pair of shoes.

Early in the morning Vicki lay with the striped sheet over her nose. Billy was on the loose in the house, a forlorn seeker. He stamped and shuffled down the hallway, in and out of rooms. He puffed and hummed as he went, he tested his voice in a series of light screams, he lapsed again into his grieving, wailing cries. He stopped outside her door. She lay still. He laughed under his breath and shoved at the door with his shoulder, grunted, gave a breathy screech, and wandered away again on dragging feet towards the room where his parents would be sitting up in their big bed reading, like two figures on a tomb. Vicki sprang up and ran across the kitchen to the bathroom. She pushed open the door. The room was not empty. She saw a rosy haze of steam pierced by bars of sunlight, a haze in which Athena – lanky legs, rounded belly, drooping breasts with pearl-grey radiating stretchmarks – was stepping out of the shower and reaching for a towel.

'Sorry!' said Vicki. She stepped back and slammed the door. She was shocked and moved, like a tourist who, bored in a gallery, has turned a corner and come face to face with a famous painting. She sat down on a kitchen chair with her towel across her lap. The window had twelve square panes. Last night's dishes stood in order in the rack.

Dexter insisted on cooking the spaghetti. He stood before the stove in a puddle of oil. The women hid in one of the bedrooms but his volleys of oaths, his tremendous singing drove them as far as the bottom of the yard.

'Morty!' he roared. 'Remember that little old lady we used to see at the Vietnam demonstrations? Must have been 1966. "Fuckin' m - u - u - urderers!" ' He burst into the drinking chorus from *La Traviata*.

'Hey Dexter!' called Vicki from the back garden. 'Come and have a look at this!'

'All right all right all *right*.' He appeared at the top of the concrete steps.

'Look at the sky!'

It was fiery down low, with scalloped yellowish clouds high up against a grey backdrop.

'Marvellous!' said Dexter. 'How do they do that? Make the smaller clouds a different colour?'

The three women stood in a row on the path and looked up at him. Their attention! He loved it. 'That's what they should have on TV every night,' he shouted. 'Not that violent American rubbish. They should have the Sunset Report. Brought to you by the Federal Department of Nature Appreciation.' He held up his wooden spoon like a wand and dropped the rest of his body into a limp arabesque. Their laughter flowed up the steps to him.

'Where's the nearest pub?' said Elizabeth. 'I'm going to buy a bottle of gin.'

Poppy brought a book. When everyone had been introduced she took the end chair and began to read with her hands round her face like blinkers.

'This is the last time I let you do this,' said Philip.

'Do what?'

'Read in company.'

'But it's boring!'

'It's rude.'

Poppy smiled and shrugged. Athena stood by the door and watched. Philip, glancing about him for support, caught her eye. He was surprised: she looked *dignified*; her limbs were narrow, her hips were wide, her hands were large and cracked. Her hair looked as if she had cut it herself, pulled it forward and chopped at it. She blushed, and he kept her glance in his and nodded several times: it might have been the courteous nod that accompanies formal introduction, except that they had already been introduced. Elizabeth strode in with an armful of bottles and a bag of ice. Vicki ran out for a lemon off the tree and cut it up. The kitchen was full of people smiling, shifting an elbow or a foot to make room, saying 'Sorry!'

[35]

'What book are you reading?' asked Arthur in his loud, sociable voice.

Poppy turned up the cover to show him.

'I've seen you on TV,' shouted Arthur.

'Who, me?' said Elizabeth.

'No, him.'

Philip shook his head. 'Couldn't have been me, mate.'

Poppy looked up from her book and directed a blank, level stare at her father.

'Yes I have!' said Arthur. 'On Countdown. You had longer hair and a sparkly shirt.'

Elizabeth laughed. 'Sparkly!' Philip dropped his head and smiled.

They began to eat.

'He doesn't actually go on TV,' said Poppy. 'He makes up songs, and he does sessions at night. Is there meat in this?'

'If you go on Countdown you get a lot of money,' said Arthur. 'They pay you a *lot* of money.'

'Oh, they do not,' said Poppy.

'Some Countdown people were making a clip in the park once,' said Arthur urgently. He was bolting his food. 'They said I might be able to go in it. They were going to pay me about two hundred dollars.'

'Bullshit,' said Poppy. 'Countdown don't make those clips. They just put them on TV.'

'I want to get one ear-ring,' said Arthur.

'Don't be silly, Arthur,' said Dexter.

'A boy at school's got one.'

'Why don't you get a tat?' said Elizabeth.

'A what?'

'A tattoo,' said Philip. He put down his fork and rolled his shirt sleeve up to his shoulder. It was a very small butterfly. Muscles and green veins rolled under his skin; his forearm was covered with fine black hairs. Arthur was so thrilled he could not speak. He gulped down the rest of his plateful. Athena could not help staring at Philip. Whenever she took her eyes away she felt him looking at her. It seemed they took it in turns.

'Have you been to America, Philip?' said Vicki.

'The sort of singer who lounges across a glass piano,' said Elizabeth.

'I like to have tortellini of a Friday,' said Philip.

'She was wearing these daggy flares,' said Elizabeth, 'with embroidered insets.'

'I got my hand jammed between two speaker boxes,' said Philip. 'My finger burst like a sausage.'

'You know?' said Vicki. 'One of those horror movies where she drives up to this house and gets dismembered?'

'I got to Reno on the bus at eight o'clock in the morning,' said Philip. 'People were stumbling about the streets in full evening dress.'

'She had all the colour and dynamism of a parsnip,' said Elizabeth. 'You could not by any stretch of the imagination drum up any feelings of sisterhood for her.'

'We've got a rabbit in a cage,' said Arthur.

'I walked in to our first gig,' said Philip, 'and they were sticking red cellophane over the lights. I thought, Oh *no*.'

'I went through centuries of torture,' said Elizabeth. 'I'd emerge exhausted from the Crusades and the Black Death only to realise that I still had to drag myself through the entire Spanish Inquisition. I never touched it again.'

'They only cost twenty-five dollars,' said Vicki, 'so I bought two pairs.'

'Does anyone want more spaghetti?' said Athena.

Dexter got up and cranked open a tin of pears.

'Sing something,' said Poppy to Elizabeth. 'Sing "Breaking Up Is Hard To Do".'

'Oh, not that,' said Philip.

'You do the come-ah come-ah,' said Elizabeth to Philip.

They sang. Billy flung himself about in Dexter's arms, loopy, with rolling eyes. Their rhythm was solid, they slid their eyes sideways to meet, and smiled as if to mock each other for their unerring harmonies. Athena saw they were professionals. The piano is such a lonely instrument, she thought: always by yourself with your back to the world. This music, thought Dexter irritably, is American music. He remembered Dr A. E. Floyd's quavering voice on the radio: 'Some people pronounce it Pur*cell*: that's an Ameddicanism.' The song ended. 'Now *we*'ll sing,' said Dexter. He put down Billy, who wandered away; he made Arthur come and stand beside his chair, and they sang 'The Wild Colonial Boy'. Arthur had the long song word-perfect. He stood to attention and threw back his head on the high notes. Vicki watched with a cold eye. 'I suppose,' thought Elizabeth, 'that he is trying to keep something alive.' It embarrassed her to see the righteous set of Dexter's mouth between verses: she looked away.

Drunk on performance, Dexter hardly let a pause fall before he cried, 'And now I'll sing "When I Survey the Wondrous Cross".' '. . . And pour contempt on aw-haw-hawl my pride,' he bawled. He drew breath and looked around him, smiling, with tear-filled eyes, his right arm still extended in its melodramatic curve. No-one spoke. Poppy turned a page.

'Mind if I sing another stanza?' he said.

'Yes,' said Vicki. 'I do. Hymns are boring.'

Had anyone ever crossed Dexter before? *Had* anyone? He jerked back as if he had been struck. His chair splintered under him and saved himself only by flexing his legs and grabbing the corner of the table with one hand.

The gin bottle was empty.

'Why was that teenager so rude to that man when he was singing?' said Poppy on the way home.

'Who knows,' said Philip.

'But I like the mother,' said Poppy. 'Athena's perfect, isn't she.'

'Perfect – you reckon?' said Philip.

Elizabeth looked at him. 'She'd have to be, to live up to the name.'

'The goddess of war,' said Philip.

'I didn't mean *that* perfect,' said Poppy.

'Of war and needlecraft,' said Elizabeth.

It was a grey rabbit. It had no name and its life was not a happy one. When Athena's parents came to visit and saw it crouched in the old chook pen half buried in Virginia creeper, her father said,

'What the hell are you keeping that for?'

'Dexter thought it would be nice for the boys,' said Athena.

'What would *he* know about rabbits. Knock it on the head. Wring its neck. Flaming pests.'

'At least in the cage by itself it can't breed,' said Athena's mother.

One morning Athena and Vicki lowered it into a deep card-board carton with grass in the bottom and a teatowel over the top, and put the box on the back seat of the car and drove it out through Footscray and down the highway.

'We'll have to get far enough away from civilisation so there won't be any feral cats,' said Vicki.

'I have to be back for the boys,' said Athena. 'I didn't mean to come this far out.'

'There's heaps of time,' said Vicki. 'We can get fish and chips. Did you bring any money? Aren't we near the sea? Go down the side road.'

There was thick grass at the verge, and a brown dam fifty feet inside the fence. Vicki knelt up on the seat and lifted the teatowel off the box. 'We should have got someone to kill it. Can Dexter kill things?'

'He killed a chook once. A dog bit the back of it right off and it was full of maggots. He held it down on a log and chopped its head off. He went white.'

They dragged the box out of the car and laid it on its side in the grass, but the rabbit would not come out. They stood waiting. The wind combed the surface of the dam into fine ridges and raised the hair on their arms.

'Is he still in there?' said Vicki. She gave the box a tap with her toe. 'Come out, come out.'

They began to giggle.

'I feel sick,' said Athena.

'Tip the box up.'

'I can't. You.'

They were convulsed with laughter. Vicki stamped her foot. Together they seized the carton and tilted its mouth to the ground. The rabbit, its ears laid back and its head withdrawn into its torso, slid towards the air. It dropped out, they whisked the box away, and it crouched shuddering between tussocks, under the huge blank sky.

❖

He should have rung up first, but he didn't have the number or the last name, and anyway that wasn't the way he did things. The back of the house was shabby, and the jasmine, whose smell he remembered from the night visit, seemed the only thing holding it together, but someone had already been working in the garden and had left neat piles of weeds all along the path to the lavatory. A row of children's tracksuit pants, frayed and dripping, hung on the line, and the bins stood with bricks on their lids at the foot of the concrete steps. All the doors and windows were open.

He made a lot of noise going in, to warn her, but the music – an orchestra, a cello – was on so loudly that she wouldn't have known if an army had marched in the back door. The passage was cool; a telephone sat on the lino. He stopped at the door through which the music poured. She was lying on her back on the floor with her eyes shut, her knees bent and her arms spread out. One foot kept the beat and her torso and her head rolled from side to side. Her face flickered and blurred like that of someone making love: a laugh relaxed into a smile, then into a vagueness as her head turned; she took a gasp of air and let it out, and all the while she rolled in time to the music, small rolls this way and that, as if she were floating on water and being lightly bobbed by a current.

He turned and walked quickly back to the kitchen, and sat on a chair and waited. The piano was open but he did not touch it straight away. He was holding his breath with embarrassment and curiosity.

She heard him out in the kitchen when the music stopped. She heard him go to the piano and plink with two fingers a tune whose name she did not know but which she had surely heard from the radio in Vicki's room. 'Tsk,' she said. 'He would play that kind of stuff.' She stepped into the passage, thinking herself safe and superior; but he struck one quiet chord, a wide blue one, a chord from the kind of music she knew nothing about and was too tight to play; she stood still, listening, and he left a silence, and then he resolved it.

How fresh and pretty he looked, sitting at her piano in his clean white shirt with the sleeves rolled up and the top button fastened! She said, 'You look gorgeous!'

He laughed and looked down. 'What was that you were listening to?'

'Haydn. It's in C major. Isn't that supposed to be the optimistic key? I could never understand why I always felt so cheerful after I'd heard that concerto, till I thought what key it was in.' She blushed: what an idiotic generalisation. Surely musicians were beyond such crassness. Nerves cause chatter. Least said soonest mended.

'Let's go somewhere?' he said.

'Where?'

'Just out. Look at things.'

'Wait till I get my bag.'

She stood in the middle of the bedroom and looked at the rows of books. She read novels fast, lying for hours on her side holding the book open on the other pillow; they blurred into one another and were gone. Great passions are ridiculous, she thought, although it is terribly cathartic to have felt. She imagined that Philip had indulged in sexual perversions with strangers. Every man she met was inferior to Dexter, but only, perhaps, because she had chosen that this should be the case.

He would have liked to move around her house and examine all its icons, or to hang over the front windowsill with her and make remarks about the dress and gait of passing pedestrians; but he wanted also to get her outside and on to his own turf, into public places where no-one was host and no-one guest, where everything had a price, where he could get what he wanted, pay for it, and keep moving in long, effortless, curving afternoons unsnagged by obligation or haste: the idea of destination meant almost as little to him as it did to Billy.

'I'm supposed to be on my way to work,' he said.

'I thought you only worked at night.'

[41]

'Something came up.'

'Are you worried about getting there on time?'

'No. I'm just worried about being comfortable.'

'Did you say "comfortable"?' said Athena.

'Yes, I did. But I didn't mean it.'

That was his way of talking. When she pressed him he was not there. Like most women she possessed, for good or ill, a limitless faculty for adjustment. She felt him give; she let herself melt, drift, take the measure of his new position, and harden again into an appropriate configuration. There was something to be got here, if only she could . . .

In the street there was a dusty summer wind, a morning not quite hot enough. If they walked shoulder to shoulder, if they sat side by side, it was in order to become the world's audience instead of being obliged to perform their personalities for each other. They bought tickets, they travelled. Their mutual curiosity was intense, but oblique. They watched one another witnessing the world: how two fat businessmen examined as merchandise the girl who pouted and pretended to read the paper in the cafe window with her skirt up round her thighs; how the waitress in Myers mural hall crossed the vast room with both arms high above her head and a dirty tablecloth hanging from each hand; the hippy boy on the tram who bought a ticket to St Kilda and announced to the other passengers, 'I must go to the sea. To the ocean'; the girl whose lips moved as she read a book called *Tortured for Christ*. The world divided itself for them, presented itself in a series of small theatrical events. 'Now,' said a woman to a man at the bus-stop, 'I'll tell you the whole story. See the thing was that . . .'

What *was* the thing? They pointed out these eventlets to each other. They did not discuss or pass judgment, but defined themselves against the attitudes revealed by the unwitting characters in these dramas. They wanted to know each other less than they wanted to agree. Harmony! To be each other. They examined clothes in shop windows.

'You could wear that jacket,' said Philip.

'I'm afraid of looking like a small man,' said Athena.

'I'm afraid of looking like an ugly woman.'

The waiter had a face like an unchipped statue. He served them in a way Philip provoked in many waiters: with delicate sideways movements he swooped the cups on to the table, and shone into Philip's eyes a smile of tender regard.

'Where does the other boy go all day?' said Philip.

Athena had to make an effort. People seemed to feel a duty to question her about this. 'To a centre. They come for him every morning in a taxi. But only during the term. He's with us all summer. Dexter and Vicki have taken him to the pool today.' Was that enough?

'Do you work, or anything? Not that I – '

'I used to. I used to – '

Two girls pushed aside the fly curtain and clacked into the cafe. They wore ear-rings like tombstones and blackish lipstick that made them look as if they had been sucking blood. Their legs were fleshless.

'Look,' said Athena. 'Look at those two. I bet they are the kind of girls you like.'

One of them stopped and leaned over the table.

'Hi, Philip!' she said, with her shoulder across Athena's face. 'Remember me?'

Her spiky hair gleamed with gel; her eyes were dots. Philip ducked his head and turned up his wrinkling smile to her, and she passed on, satisfied. She and her friend arranged themselves at the next table, well within Philip's eye-line. To Athena they looked very young, and rapacious.

'Sorry I couldn't introduce you,' said Philip. 'I've forgotten . . .'

'Are you famous?' said Athena. She laughed.

Philip's afternoon lurched in its tracks, and righted itself. 'Better ask Elizabeth that,' he said.

Poppy vacuumed the living room carpet and stacked the newspapers under the sink. When Elizabeth came they would go into Campion and buy her school textbooks secondhand.

Poppy could not understand the mentality of kids who under-
lined their books and wrote stupid comments in biro: she
longed for brandnew books, their glossy modern pages and
luscious smell, but there was no point in going on about it. Even
her uniform was secondhand. At the end of last term, Philip
took her to the new school, Clever Girls' High as he insisted on
calling it, even out loud on the tram, and they were guided to a
great big barn with no windows and a concrete floor where
other girls' mothers, in aprons and tight perms, helped them
sort through mounds of grey pleated skirts, gingham dresses
and red jumpers, looking for the right size, which in Poppy's
case was so extremely small that she was ashamed, and her
shame mingled with the admiration and vanity she always felt
at being in public places with her father, who was different
from everyone else's, younger-looking and not a dag, and he
talked slowly and quietly to people, looking them right in the
eye and not doing false laughter with workers like other fathers
she had seen. There was, on the trestle table, one last pleated
skirt small enough, and Philip got his hand on it a split second
before the mother of the only other very short girl, who cast at
Poppy a glance of complicated camaraderie and relief: now
she, not Poppy, would have to buy a new one in a proper shop
with mirrors and fitting rooms, and the pleats would still be
tacked together round the hem and it would smell clean, not
op-shoppy and doggy and wet-jumpery like all the uniforms in
this gloomy building with the swinging light bulbs and the
canteen price lists still on the wall from the year that had just
finished.

Poppy went into her bedroom and put on the uniform. She
did this at least once a day, to practise getting used to it, and
because she could not quite believe, from one day to the next,
in its extreme ugliness. Worst were the shoes, great black
lace-up clod-hoppers with square toes. Would they ever get
soft? She stood in front of the mirror in the hall and stared at
her brown, stick-like legs and long feet. Elizabeth came in
behind her. Her eyes too were drawn to these boat-like extremities. They reminded her of the ankleboots worn by Ant
and Bee in a book her mother had read to her. She thought of
her mother and the sight of Poppy's anxiety made her voice
tremble.

'Head prefect of Mosquito Girls' High,' she said.

Poppy turned round with a crooked smile. She took the bait. 'I know what!' she said. 'Let's write a story. Let's start like this: "Things were buzzing at Mosquito Girls' High".'

'The headmistress's name is Miss Queenie Bee,' said Elizabeth.

'And she says to all the girls at assembly, "If there's one thing that really bugs me . . ."'

'And no-one wants to be the school swot. Swat, get it?'

They pranced and frolicked in the hall. Elizabeth got bored with it long before Poppy did.

'Come on,' she said. 'Let's get this show on the road. Did Shithead leave you any money for the stuff?'

'No,' said Poppy. 'He said for you to pay and tell him how much.'

They sat in the high seats at the back of the bus, and Poppy sank into her book. Up at the front sat a European woman in her forties, dressed in a satin suit and high-heeled shoes as if for an outing. Elizabeth could not work out her relationship to the two men she appeared to be with, who were conversing in the seat opposite. As the bus swung round into Russell Street, one of the men tossed a piece of screwed-up paper on to the high shelf of the woman's breasts. She looked down very slowly, and very slowly she picked the rubbish off her bosom; she was smiling with humiliation. Elizabeth stood up to walk down the bus to the door, with Poppy stumbling after her, still reading. The woman looked up at Elizabeth as she passed. They held eyes. The woman made the grimace, and Elizabeth returned it: corners of the mouth go down, head tilts to one side, shoulders come up in a shrug: *are they worth it?* It was a secret showing of badges, of scars. Had Poppy seen? It would contaminate her. But Poppy was finishing a chapter. She kept a grip on Elizabeth's sleeve and forged down the page with her eyes. Her feet were braced well apart on the jolting floor.

They found the textbooks and paid for them, but Poppy lingered to admire the blocky reams of paper and the silver bulldog clips clamped into a chain. Elizabeth picked up a handsome bound diary.

'This is reduced,' she said. 'I'll buy it.'

They stood by the register, but the boy serving would not

come. Minutes passed. Poppy lounged and read on. Elizabeth observed that the diary was invisible in her arms among their already wrapped purchases. The adrenalin squirted and twinkled in her veins. *Oh! did I forget to pay for this one? Sorry! You kept us waiting for so long! How much is it again?* 'Come on,' she said to Poppy in an ordinary voice, and walked quickly towards the door.

'*Elizabeth!*' said Poppy.

'Shutup!' she hissed. She barged out on to the bright street. Poppy trotted after her, keeping her finger in the book to mark her place, and caught up with her half a block away. Elizabeth was panting. She sat down on the deep window ledge of a furniture shop and pulled the furious girl to face her. 'Now don't you *ever* do what I just did,' she said.

'*Me?*' said Poppy. 'It's got nothing to do with *me!*'

'You're such a puritan!' said Elizabeth. 'You make me feel like a criminal.'

'You *are* a criminal. Taking other people's stuff is wrong.'

'You should talk! What about that camera.'

Poppy held her book to her chest. 'That was different. Finding things is not the same as stealing them.'

'You could've reported it.'

'I will, then,' said Poppy. 'I'll take it back.'

'Don't be pathetic. It was years ago – you don't even remember which motel it was.'

'It was one of them. On that highway.'

'It's too late now.'

They were both red and breathing hard. They stared away from each other, their arms folded round their possessions. Cars passed. The asphalt was spongy.

'We'll both burn in hell,' said Elizabeth.

'I don't believe in hell.'

'We'll burn somewhere else, then.'

'Are you going to keep the diary?'

'Are you going to keep the camera?'

'I might. Or I might not. I might . . . donate it to charity.'

'They'd know it was hot. People don't give away good stuff that works.'

Elizabeth waited. Poppy stood up and brushed off the seat of her pants. 'All right,' she said. 'Let's go to Allans. I feel like playing the pianos.'

The house of music was lumbered with grands, a noble line of them, each fluttering a many-digited price tag. Their lids were propped open as if to catch a breath of air. Their perfect teeth, their glossy flanks, their sumptuous smell caused customers to tiptoe past them on their way to the secondhand uprights at the back; but Poppy fronted up to a big black Bösendorfer and settled herself on the bench. She handed her book to Elizabeth, wiped her palms on her thighs and launched into something that used all her fingers.

'That's a lovely piece of music, that is!' sang out a young salesman who was sitting at a Steinway, five juggernauts down the line.

She stumbled, she paused to listen to him. He picked it up and played the next two bars. He waited for her, poising his hands above the keys and raising his eyebrows. She hesitated, with a glance and a smile at Elizabeth, and then she skated away into the elements. Their game was clever: the man teased, the girl echoed him, they were flirting with each other, laughing; they played three slow chords in unison. People stopped and listened, pretending not to, because it was so intimate. Elizabeth wandered away to the head of the stairs. From the lower regions the grim thumping of an electric bass rolled up and throbbed in the metal banisters.

❖

Vicki spent an hour getting herself ready. She tied a diaphanous scarf round her head, stuck a yellow rose in it, and put a lot of makeup on her flat, smooth, pale face. She looked striking, and flustered because of the lipstick she had rubbed into her cheekbones.

'One thing you can be sure of,' said Dexter in the car. 'No-one else in the place will be dressed like you.'

How would you know, thought Vicki; you never go to any

places. 'Why don't you ever wear makeup, Thena?' she said.

'Athena doesn't believe in makeup,' said Dexter. 'Do you dear. She's got beautiful skin.'

'I don't know how to put it on,' said Athena.

'You don't need it, dear,' said Dexter.

'I wouldn't mind a bit of feminine mystique, once in a while,' said Athena.

'You don't want that rubbish,' said Dexter.

Athena sat beside him in the front seat with straight spine and folded hands. It alarmed Vicki to see her shoulders tremble with holding back. 'Elizabeth used to be against make-up,' she chattered. 'But now she even puts polish on her toe-nails. She says, "I've made my reputation as a strong woman. I reckon I've earned the right to a couple of red blobs on my extremities."'

Athena laughed. 'She's clever, isn't she.'

'A bit too clever, sometimes,' said Dexter. He waltzed the car from lane to lane with big flourishes of the steering wheel. 'I can't even remember the last time we went dancing. Will you have a dance with me, Vicki?'

'Dexter!' she said. 'Nobody dances *with* anybody any more!'

'Have they started already?' said Athena at the door.

'No,' said Vicki. 'It's just a tape.'

'Can't they turn it down a bit?' said Dexter.

Elizabeth saw them from the bar where she and Philip were leaning while the other band packed up. 'She's brought her mum and dad,' she said.

Philip turned round. 'Looks embarrrassed, doesn't she.'

'Wouldn't you? Get the look on his face.'

'I like him,' said Philip. 'He's like a character out of a Russian novel, or a Wagner opera. A noble soul.'

'A what?'

'He's the coolest person here. He's not even trying.'

'You're not kidding. That shirt. It's like a pyjama top.'

Vicki skidded up to the bar beside them.

'Cute scarf,' said Philip.

'Reckon?' said Vicki with a triumphant glance at Elizabeth. She ordered a Kahlua and milk.

'What's that stuff?' said Dexter. 'I'll get us a jug. Anyone want to share a jug?'

[48]

'I'm drinking whisky,' said Elizabeth.

'I'll have one too,' said Athena.

'This whole place is painted black,' said Dexter. 'It's like a vision of hell.'

'Shutup, Dexter,' said Vicki. 'Don't be so *loud*.'

'This isn't a proper glass,' said Dexter. 'Here, mate – you've given me a plastic glass.'

The barman, who had two false plaits twined into his hair at the back, shrugged and served the next person.

'For safety,' said Philip. He nodded at Dexter and turned his mouth down at the corners. What if I told him about the headbangers, he thought; he wouldn't believe me. Philip downed his drink and walked away: the crowd parted for him.

Safety! Dexter stood holding the plastic glass of beer and stared around him. These kids didn't look as if they would smash glass. They had cold, passionless faces. He knew the phrase for it: '*l' inébranlable résolution de ne pas être ému.*' They were like refugees, war orphans, thronging in their drab clothes. It was too late to get out. The big room was packed solid and he was backed up against the bar. He looked for Athena, to mention the Baudelaire to her. She was emptying her glass in one swig, and her face was already turned towards the stage which at that moment went black.

Vicki kept her eyes on the dark patch, and saw the pale blur of Philip's shirt, the faint shapes of the musicians creeping out, stepping over leads, fumbling with their instruments. Light and sound burst as one and she saw the shock wave hit Dexter: his eyes became slits and he turned his head this way and that like a baby with ear-ache. Vicki charged down the front to dance beside girls she did not know but who meet her eye and smile at her as they leap and bob and twirl about in their cheap and cheerful dresses, in the brief camaraderie of moving to music. They are happy! They are laughing ! They are young and silly and here to have fun!

Athena worked her way forward as far as the front row of non-dancers. She was blasted by noise but fired with curiosity. She could not tell which instrument was producing which sound, but she heard a guitar playing something that started as casually as water spilling over the lip of a basin and wondered if it was proceeding from Philip's fingers; she heard a boy behind

[49]

her roar to his friend, 'They're a bit *guitary*, aren't they?'; she saw the fat-hipped keyboard player raise his wrists up high and move his lips like a slow reader; and with a piercing envy she saw Philip's sociable demeanour, his raised head, his skipping turns, and the glances, the smiles of a tender complicity that passed between him and the others as they drowned themselves in sound.

At the first break Dexter forced his way through the shoulders to Athena and seized her elbow at the very moment her other arm was taken by Vicki fighting towards the bar. Vicki was glassy and smiling, Dexter frowning and wild-eyed. In their linked, three-way posture they might have been performing a country dance.

'Let's get out of here!' shouted Dexter. 'Those aren't instruments! They're machines!'

A passing boy sneered. Vicki's face closed. 'I'll get a lift home,' she said.

'I think I'd like to stay too, Dex,' said Athena.

Betrayed, Dexter did not argue. 'I'll wait for you in the car,' he said, and ploughed away to the door.

Dexter stumbled out past the posters into the hotel carpark. It was a mild summer night. A warm wind puffed now and then, a wind that had passed across the river and through miles of suburban gardens, across the roofs of houses in which lived people's aunties, and doctors, and university professors, and adults and children whose families had put them into institutions. He had not drunk enough. The music was nothing to him now but a dulled thudding, though his head was ringing. How did the neighbours put up with it? He unlocked the car door and got in. His wide, short trouser leg snagged on the door handle. The inside of the car comforted him. He could smell his children in it, their grubbiness, their chip packets; and something else, something more than a smell, a faint fleshiness which was evidence that his wife had been there. Even Vicki's strident perfume could not swamp it. He picked it up as surely as a nesting bird recognises its mate's cry in the dense cacophony of an Antarctic island. Sometimes if he went to the lavatory after her he smelled it so strongly that it almost revolted him: it was his mother's smell, sickeningly rich and warm, an emanation from internal membranes.

What was that noise? He wound the window right down and stuck his head out. Someone was sobbing in the carpark, a woman, a girl. She was wailing, choking, trying to talk. He pulled his head in and went for the door handle but the moronic thumping of the music stopped dead and a man's voice spoke, light, reasoning, impatient.

'Look, Donna,' it said, 'why can't you just accept it? And make the best of it?'

'But you don't – you never – I can't – ' She was weeping without shame. They were standing in the dark behind Dexter's car. He heard the man click his tongue and sigh, then the sobbing became muffled. He's put his arms around her, thought Dexter, but he doesn't love her any more. He rolled up the window as quietly as he could, although his urge to go on listening was almost sexual. His heart was beating. The music began again, stamp, stamp, stamp. The girl's grief passed through metal and glass and became part of Dexter. His cells were sodden with it. He would carry it forever, long after she had recovered from it and gone on to love someone else.

Beside one of the speaker boxes crouched an androgynous creature in a raincoat. Its neck was bent, its hair was slicked back like a schoolboy's off its sweating, waxen face, it nodded its head in time and kept its eyes turned up sideways and fixed on the lit, jerking figures above it. Something damned in its posture and its crooked stare made Athena shiver. She followed it to the lavatory – so it was a girl – and heard it vomiting.

She found Elizabeth standing watching the band from the side. The music stopped.

'Did you see that girl? Is she all right?'

'I saw a thing in a raincoat,' said Elizabeth, 'with no features on its face.'

'She was vomiting. Do you think I ought to do something?'

'What – clean up? They hire people to do that.'

'But she looked like a child.'

'They all do,' said Elizabeth. 'They *are*.'

The girl emerged, paler than before, and slithered back to

her crouching position of worship, or supplication. Athena noticed that from where Elizabeth was standing, Philip looked . . . famous. From below the stage, where Athena had spent most of the evening, he had looked like a bloke with a guitar doing a job of work.

When Athena opened the passenger door at midnight she found Dexter asleep with his head on his arms, and his arms on the steering wheel. He did not move, though people were shouting and laughing and starting up cars all around. She stood bent over, half in and out of the car, and looked at his face from the side. She found it pretty. It wasn't, but that was how she saw it. She thought, 'You will never be anything to me but beautiful.' She slid in beside him and he woke.

'Hullo, dearest!' he said. 'All over, is it?' He stretched his arms backwards and arched his spine.

'It was fun,' said Athena. 'We've been dancing and dancing.'

'I had a wonderful stroke of luck,' said Dexter. 'I turned on the wireless and they were playing that Mozart clarinet quintet, you know, the one I like so much?' He pursed his lips and whistled a rising run of notes, one forefinger lifted like a prophet. 'It's sublime. Beyond praise! Where's Vicki?'

'She said she'd be home later,' said Athena.

They lay wide awake, smelling the summer night, restless, involved in their separate travellings, longing to slip off the edge into real sleep.

'Are you still awake?' said Athena.

'Yes.'

'Stop thinking. How can I drop off next to a head full of thoughts?'

[52]

Dexter got up with a sigh. She heard his bare feet brush on the hall lino, and stretched out into the cool corners of the bed. What time could it be? Her feet felt dry-skinned and feverish. Her hair stank of other people's cigarette smoke. She turned the pillow over and over. A door creaked, someone laughed up high, there was a scuffling somewhere in the house, Dexter was up, he would see to it. Her muscles let go and she was away.

Someone was whispering above her head, through the window, tap tap tap on glass, calling her name. Her feet hit the floor and her finger the lamp switch before her eyes were open. 'What? What?'

'Come and open the front door, Thena! It's me!'

'What on earth are you doing?' Dexter was standing on the front verandah in his pyjamas with both hands clapped over his mouth and his eyes rolling. He scampered past her and dived on to the bed.

'He had her up against the fridge!' he snorted. He giggled and thrashed his legs like a naughty boy in a dormitory. 'I was on my way to the lavatory. I turned on the kitchen light and they were – '

'Who?' She pushed the bedroom door to and flicked off the light.

'Him! The one with the tattoo! He had his trousers off, in the kitchen!'

'What? Is Elizabeth here!'

'No! It was Vicki! I had to come back round the outside of the house. They must have thought I was perving on them.' He took a big quivering breath. 'Is there going to be a scandal?'

'Isn't she a little monkey,' said Athena. 'I hope she's on the pill.' She lay down, smiling to herself. The curtain moved on the air, settled, moved again. It was like waiting for a play to continue.

An engine slowed down outside, a taxi radio quacked, a door slammed, heels clacked to the verandah as smartly as if it were broad day.

'Here's your scandal,' said Athena.

They lay flinching on the bed. Her knocking shook the house. The neighbour's dog began to bark.

'Open the door,' said Athena. 'She'll wake the kids.'

He scrambled into the hall. Elizabeth pushed past him and

charged down the hall towards Vicki's room.

'The back door wasn't locked, Morty,' Dexter sang out after her. 'She'll think it's our fault,' he hissed to Athena.

'Don't be silly. Let them sort it out for themselves.' She turned her back to him and he flung his arm around her.

'This is awful!' he said.

'This must be what people *do*,' said Athena. 'Go to sleep.'

Dexter lay rigid as a board, braced for more sobbing, but Athena slept, and dreamed that she was in a garden, on a large, flat, well-kept lawn, where yellow leaves off poplars lay about in drifts. As she watched they began to rise off the grass and play in the air in orderly streams as if being squirted from a hose: they rose and fell and rose again, in a variety of patterns, and everything was beautiful and enchanting and as it should be.

❖

They stood in the shade on the cool tiles of an arcade and looked into a shop window where an automatic photo printing machine was on display. Before their eyes it disgorged into the chute a single colour snap: a baby in a humidicrib. As one they turned away.

'I used to play my guitar all day at home,' said Philip. 'I used to think that if people could hear these certain notes played at this certain rhythm, then they'd understand everything and everything would change.'

'Do you feel horrible,' said Athena, 'when you've played less well than you ought to have? And exposed yourself?'

'I used to,' said Philip. 'I used to go looking for heroin or dope or a lot of whisky so I could get oblivious as fast as I could. Because of shame. And wanting to wipe out this person and be nothing. Not just after I've played badly either. When I've behaved like an animal. Hurting people. These last few mornings I've been shaving and I've looked in the mirror and thought, I could pull the razor across here like this' – he drew a line from ear to ear – 'except that it would hurt so much.'

'And make such a mess,' said Athena. 'I think of jumping off buildings.'

'Jumping, do you?' He was alarmed.

'I don't mean I want to die,' said Athena. 'I just get that feeling, when I stand on a high balcony, that I'd like to jump out into the air.'

He nodded.

'Do you ever think it might be true?' said Athena.

'What?'

'Hell, and all that.'

He grabbed the back of her hair in a bunch and tugged at it. He looked upset. 'No. No, I don't.' He kept his hand on her shoulder and then slipped it back into his pocket. 'Will we go and walk round in Georges?'

'I haven't got any money,' said Athena.

'I can lend you some. They finally paid me.'

'I'm not going to buy anything.'

'Here. Just to hold. Fifty dollars to keep in your pocket till you get to the bank. So you won't be bereft.'

The note was new. Its surface was oily and it had a military smell, like calico. He went on ahead of her. 'Ten minutes, at the corner.'

She looked at some jeans, the kind Vicki wore that she had to lie on her back to zip up. She went to the bank and took out the money for the food shopping. On her way to the meeting place she planned what she would say to him when she gave him back his money. In a light voice she would say, 'Here you are, my sweetheart, my darling, my treasure.' She would get the tone just right. Her heart was beating. She got to the corner and stopped outside the bra shop. He was not there. The dry wind fluffed out her hair like koala's ears.

❖

Dexter was out when Elizabeth and Poppy came in through the back gate. Athena, sitting on the concrete step in the evening, did not think she could entertain them on her own without the screen of his noisy sociability. She had wasted half the day wandering in the city with Philip, it was late, and she should have been, she should be . . . But the girl was carrying a cello in a case.

'We came to ask a favour,' said Elizabeth. She pushed Poppy forward. 'Go on. You ask.'

'I have to go to my music lesson,' said Poppy. 'My father forgot. He went off in the car and I haven't got any way of getting there.'

'Do you want me to drive you?' said Athena.

They were embarrassed, having meant to ask Dexter.

'It's straight out the freeway,' said Poppy.

'She can show you the way,' said Elizabeth.

'It's my last one for the year,' said Poppy. 'It's already paid for.'

Athena got to her feet.

'Do you want me to come?' said Elizabeth.

Everyone understood the meaning of this question.

'Last summer,' she said, 'I went to the concert hall when Poppy played in the music camp orchestra. I took one look at those rows and rows of skinny legs and enormous Adidas runners going tap tap tap and I burst into tears.'

'Elizabeth doesn't like orchestras much,' said Poppy. 'She doesn't like quite a few things.'

'Opera.'

'Cheese.'

'Tracksuits.'

They pantomimed themselves for her, struck dramatic poses and exaggerated their elocution. She watched them, and looked for the father in the child. He showed himself only fleetingly: the colour was wrong, the cheeks were rounder, but she saw his jawline and the secretiveness of the smile.

'Hop in the car, Poppy,' said Athena. 'I'll whip these sheets off the line before it gets dark.'

The girl obeyed. She arranged the cello on the back seat and leaned forward to the dashboard so she could watch the two women approach the wire and unpeg the sheets. They faced each other, joined by the cloth, and raised their arms in unison, they shook the cloth and snapped it tight, they advanced and retreated until each sheet was a flat bundle in Athena's arms. Poppy saw that they were speaking, with pauses, but she could not hear what they were saying.

'Philip came to see me,' said Athena.

'To see *you*.'

'A couple of times.'

Elizabeth laughed with closed lips. 'Take you for walks, did he?'

'Yes.'

'Do you like him?'

'Yes.'

'He's always looking for new blood. Something new. A little thrill for that amusement park he calls his mind.'

Their fingers met formally at the high corners of the sheet. Elizabeth's relinquished, Athena's accepted. As they folded, as they spoke, the light left the garden.

The teacher opened the door. He had a red pencil between his teeth and his feet were bare.

'The *Herald's* on the kitchen table,' he said, 'if you want to wait out there.'

Athena unfolded the paper. They went round the corner on to the flowery carpet and out of her sight. They left the door ajar.

'What can you tell me about Mozart?' said the teacher.

'Nothing.'

'Come on.'

'He was a composer.'

'Right. What else? How old was he when he gave his first concert?'

'Six?'

'About that. He was a bit crazy. Did you know that?'

'No.'

'Yeah. He was a bit crazy. Too clever. Too bright. Have you practised?'

'A bit.'

'A bit. We'll see about that. We'll start with this.'

'Oh. I didn't know I was going to play that for you. But I'll play it anyway.'

'I don't want any honkytonk, understand? I want 'em all smooth. Hold up that hand nicely. Bend that thumb. Away you go.'

Athena opened the glass door and sat on the kitchen step with her feet on the gravel. The big back yard was dark, but women were talking in quiet voices, perhaps in the garage, or on the verandah of the house next door. Somewhere in the garden there was a large bush of daphne. Over there must be Essendon. A plane was coming down, too far away for her to hear.

She was cold. She slid the door shut and went back to the table. Now the teacher was playing too. His vibrato was steady and confident. Poppy wavered, but kept going. She was game. He bellowed at her.

'Scrub at it a bit more! Get a nice meaty tone! Go back to B. B, ya sausage! Not B flat! Sounds like you're swinging a cat round by the tail. Don't just throw in the towel! You gotta keep going!'

'Where am I? I don't know where I am!'

'Strike a light. Look, Poppy. What does it say here? What's written here? *Dolce*. What's that mean? Sweetly. Not like a monster. Flat! You're flat as a tack.'

'It's wrong. I'm playing it wrong.'

'It's riddled with mistakes, like a piece of cheese. It's never all right. There's always something wrong.'

'Well what's the use of playing, then?'

'Hmmm. *At the stage you're at*, there's always something wrong. Later . . . that comes from experience. You must have some patience. Do you know what patience is?'

'Yeah. Not being in a hurry. Waiting.'

'That's it. Take your time. Don't get worried and upset. Take your time and work it out. Look at each individual trouble spot and analyse *why* it's giving you trouble. See? There's an explanation to it, isn't there? Don't think I'm not pleased with you. I am. Now we'll play together. You do the bottom line, OK? Lightly, sweetly – two three *four*.'

Like many women of her age whose opinions, when they were freshly thought and expressed, had never received the attention they deserved, Mrs Fox had slid away into a habit of monologue, a stream of mild words which concealed the bulk of thought and knowledge as babbling water hides submerged boulders. She was the kind of private-minded, endlessly good-humoured woman whose sons, even in their twenties and in fact until they married, had brought home from other states suitcases full of dirty clothes for her to wash; the kind of woman who, when Doctor Fox, almost tiptoeing with reverence, put on his record of the Goldberg Variations, could cheerfully whisper to the nineteen-year-old Elizabeth, working beside her at the sink, 'Variations? They all sound the same to me!' Arthur, who reminded her of the young Dexter in his garrulous social confidence, his unsinkable all-knowingness, loved to make up wondrous tales of her adventures.

'Vicki,' he said in the kitchen, 'did you know that Iris used to be an interpreter in Germany during the war?'

'Did she?' said Vicki. Rapid mental arithmetic would have reassured her, had she been more certain of the dates of the second world war, that this could not be true: Iris was having children in Melbourne during the war.

'Oh yes,' said Arthur. He curved his clever scissors in and out of a sheet of paper, cutting out helmets. 'She was an interpreter for the Germans. She used to question people.'

'*Question* people?'

Arthur saw her face drop and went on smoothly, 'There were no executions, though. They were all found to be farmers.'

The blades opened and closed, crunched through the paper.

'I might go out,' said Vicki.'People's parents never like me.'

'My parents do,' said Arthur.

'Older parents, I meant,' said Vicki.

'They might wonder exactly what you're doing here,' said Arthur. 'In our spare room.'

'What do *you* think I'm doing here?'

He bent his smiling face over his work. 'Well – you have to live somewhere, don't you.'

'Don't you like me living here?'

He pulled the box of Derwents towards him and flipped back the lid. 'I'm going through a period of self-conscience,' he said. 'I haven't really thought about it.'

They came in carrying things: a bunch of flowers, a tin of anzacs, a parcel in brown paper which Mrs Fox handed to Athena. She began to unwrap it. The stickytape popped.

'It's an iron,' said Athena.

She pulled the cardboard and the packing off it and took hold of the pale plastic handle. The cord was brown, flecked with blue, and was tightly wound in a rubber band.

'We've already got an iron, haven't we dear,' said Dexter.

'This is a good iron, though,' said Athena. 'Ours is old.'

'I knew you had a lot of clothes to iron,' said Mrs Fox. 'I saw this in Myers. I was on my way through to the layby department and I saw it there and I thought I'll get that for Athena, I know what it's like when the shirts pile up, not to mention tablecloths and so on, so I bought it. There's a guarantee card in the box, you should fill it out and send it back to them straight away, just in case there's something wrong with it.'

'Athena doesn't do all that much ironing,' said Dexter.

Athena held the iron at arm's length, raised it and lowered it as if to test its weight. 'It's a very good iron,' she said.

'I love to see the creases in their little pyjama pants,' said Mrs Fox.

Dexter took the iron. 'It's so light!' he said. 'How could you make things flat with that? Irons should be *heavy*.'

The women looked at each other. Athena folded the brown paper and put it away in a drawer.

'When I was at boarding school,' said Dexter, 'there was a boy called Robert, a miserable kid with no friends – spots, pimples, bad breath, hopeless at sport. One day it was his fifteenth birthday, and a parcel came for him from his parents. For once people were interested in him. We gathered round to watch him open his present. And in it there was a safety razor and a packet of blades.'

'I don't get it,' said Arthur.

'It's not meant to be funny, Arthur,' said Mrs Fox.

'Is there someone out in your back yard?' said Doctor Fox. He was not able to sit still in a room, but must always be pacing about peering at things, riffling through bills on the shelf, staring for an unnecessarily long time at a postcard tacked to the wall. Now he was pressing his face against the window and squinting into the afternoon sun.

'There is someone out there,' he said. 'Behind those bushes.'

'Probably one of the Papantuano kids,' said Dexter.

'No. It's a girl. Good lord. She's half naked. She *is* naked. It's a young savage.'

'It's Vicki,' said Athena. 'Sunbaking.'

'Who's Vicki?' said Mrs Fox.

'Remember Morty?' said Dexter. 'Her sister. She's living with us. At the moment.'

Doctor Fox came away from the window and sat down with his back to the piano. ' "This is the present Mrs Harris",' he said with a naughty look at Athena. ' "My first wife is up there." Who wrote that?'

'James Thurber,' said Dexter.

Arthur squeezed in beside Doctor Fox on the piano bench. He turned up his face and said in a fond voice, 'I love sitting next to you, Grandpa.'

'Do you?' said the old man. He was surprised.

They all walked out on the summer afternoon. The men took Arthur to bowl and bat, deep in the park near the drinking fountain, but the women kept going, with Billy between them, as far as the big cemetery and in through the turnstile. Billy's hands sweated in theirs. Inside the railings the world opened out. The horizon widened and dropped away, and the sky rose until there was nothing above them but dry air: they crept along a plateau that tilted slightly to the south-east, in which

[61]

direction lay many suburbs and a low mountain, very far.

Mrs Fox's discourse ceased while she took account of this immensity of air, lowness of ground, distantness of landmarks. Then it began again, and wound on and on through the afternoon, stupefying in its pointlessness and yet as soothing, as voluptuous as the murmuring of a dressmaker, the warm-handed whisperer who kneels in contemplation before the hem, who pats and strokes, bunches and gathers, in whose presence nothing is required but perfect passivity.

Cars were parked on the curving bitumen roads inside the walls. Their boots were open, and dark teenagers, obedient but blank-faced, trotted to and from the taps with plastic buckets of water, serving their parents who worked slowly and silently at the graves, sweeping, polishing, decorating, making ready.

'Some of those graves haven't even got anyone in them,' said Athena.

'You never know,' said Mrs Fox. 'You never know what's going to happen.'

They walked to tire the boy. He was quiet, and kept up easily, clumping along in his heavy shoes. From time to time he swung his head back and let out a whinny of laughter.

They wandered for a long time. When they got back to the gate through which they had entered, it was chained and padlocked. The turnstile was high and crowned with barbed wire. The flower seller had closed her kiosk and gone home. The path was empty of cars. The bins were stuffed with paper and dry flower stalks.

'You'd think they could at least ring a bell,' said Mrs Fox. 'Like they do at the Botanic Gardens.'

'There are always a few railings missing,' said Athena. 'Let's walk round the edge till we find one.'

They set off at a brisk pace. They walked so smartly that the cast-iron railings rippled in the corner of their field of vision. Cyclists outside, free to pedal home for tea, flickered by like subliminal suggestions.

'They must have mended the fences,' said Athena.

They passed nuns' graves, hosts of flat grey slabs under cypress trees. Nut-like things had dropped from the trees' bony branches, and lay in clusters where a slab had shifted and made a hollow. Other graves were quite abandoned; their

it. Her clothes hang off her, but her husband's and her children's are still clean and ready. She starts to walk by herself at night, she can hardly wait to be out of the house, they cannot seize her attention once the sun has set, her eyes will wander away to the open door, and Dexter knows he is not invited. She comes back after they have gone to sleep, and yet wakes before them. Her sexual life is solitary: she comes to visions of meadows full of flowers, white ones floating like a cloud above tangled green stalks, or to visions of great machines, or of galleries, endless, with high deep windows and velvet curtains and noble pieces of furniture, leather-trimmed, Florentine galleries along which her disembodied consciousness progresses to a stately pulse. She lies on dry grass in parks, she falls asleep for seconds and wakes thinking she is in her bed and that the wind on her face has come in through the open window. On breathless summer evenings, when men in white trousers loll in doorways, she goes alone to the Paradise, and to the throbbing of the strange music there, the tangos, stern, passionate, intellectual music, the waiter kisses her on the mouth and glides away. In some other stifling bar at midnight the Italians set down their cues and turn in mid-breath to the TV set high above the doorway: 'Oh! ah!' she cries with them, watching the Olympic skier flash, lime-green, alone and perfect, over the whiteness, somewhere on the other side of the world. She passes a lane in which a pale disc shimmers, a man's face, her stomach oozes; he lunges, he takes hold of her, she smells his breath, she opens her mouth to scream and yes! she screams! It is not a woman's dream where she stretches wide but cannot utter: she kicks him, her foot meets bone, she throws his arms back, she screams so loudly and so well that a car stops, doors fly open, people run shouting to her aid. She opens the back gate, can it be still the same summer night? and finds they have dragged their mattresses out into the garden for the heat and are sleeping under the dimming stars, heedless of dew, with sheets drawn over their heads against the mosquitoes. She chooses Arthur, finds him, fits herself to the hard beads of his spine, smells his stalky neck, hears from under the fig tree the tireless scraping of a cricket. The first train, a row of lit boxes, clatters empty over the Merri bridge. Arthur stirs, flings up one arm, shrugs her off. The early wind brings a branch crashing down off one of the elms along the creek: she hears it rustle and thump. The same wind moves in the hall and turns over a page of the telephone directory. She sits at Dexter's table. An orange rests on his papers to prevent them from blowing away. Under the round beam of the planet lamp she mends with stickytape a torn dollar note. At dawn Dexter stumbles in and stands looking at her. She thinks, I can't be bothered fucking if it's going to be obscure. But she does, they do, and the familiarity of his breathing by her ear brings up a rush of violence in her like vomiting: she pushes at his face with her flat palm, seizes a handful of his hair and drags at it, beside herself; but their torsos continue to move smoothly, their habit imperturbable, and just as she comes she sees a coin of sun on the puffing bulge of the lace curtain and bursts out sobbing.

❖

'You're pretty crazy, aren't you,' said Philip. 'I have to go to Sydney. Better come with me. I'll pay.'

Perhaps there was a world where people could act on whims, where deeds could detach themselves cleanly from all notion of consequences. Perhaps this never-quite-present Philip might be that mythical creature, a man who was utterly scrupulous and who was yet prepared to do anything. Perhaps she too might never apologise, never explain.

The taxi came. She looked back as it drove away, and saw Dexter standing on the front verandah in his old tartan dressing gown, bare-shinned, holding the paper in his hand. Arthur was beside him. Their faces, shocked, floated after her like two balloons on a string. One could behave like this only by numbing something, and the skin of the body, as if to compensate, peeled back and laid bare the nerves.

Even the route he took to the airport was new to her. They went by Melville Road and Bell Street, they came over the rise

[65]

and rolled down the hill and there it was! the freeway flying away in all directions! Her own city was cracked open for her, as neatly as a nut opens at one tap of a hammer. From the plane window she thought she saw a rabbit tearing madly along beside the runway, but perhaps it was only the shadow of the wing.

'This hotel is a dump,' said Philip. 'I love it.' He turned on the television and lay on the bed. She was ashamed of her motherly body, of the homely uses to which it had been put, of the marks of its unromantic experience. But then, in curiosity, she forgot to think, and when she rolled over, the sky behind her back had turned orange. They slept, they woke. 'Fucking you,' he said, 'is like having a long and interesting conversation.' His expressions changed, and changed. He laughed, he swore, he became distracted, he closed his eyes: tears fell from his eyes, he wiped them away impatiently. He seized her attention with his eyes, sucked her into his eyes. But late in the morning he drew himself together, neatly took his cock out of her, and got off the bed.

'Now I have to make some phone calls,' he said.

Everything was his idea: things he proposed they did, and he paid. He knew where places were and how to get there. He showed her: taxis, a rented Commodore to the ocean in the early evening. He wore a creased suit over a T-shirt, he spent money as fast as he got it, he slid the plastic card across counters with his wrinkling smile, tellers ate from his hand. They walked to the water where in sunny air metal clinked above moored yachts. They passed a beautiful house of Italian squareness and ochreness, and flatness of gravel and barredness of window and thickness of foliage by the gate.

'Will you ever have a house like that, Philip?'

'Nnnn . . . Yes. I will.'

They walked along the watery edge of the Botanic Gardens; they looked at the nuns, the sails, the eggshells of the Opera House. 'Patriotic, isn't it,' he said.

She slept, he did not seem to need to. He went to work. She could not imagine what his work entailed, what he did, and tried to piece it together from his random remarks, without showing her ignorance.

'You put everything you can think of in at the beginning,' he said, 'and then you start taking bits out.'

'But how can you take bits of music off a tape, once you've . . .'

'There are . . .' Philip was patient. 'Well – you've got twenty-four tracks, right?'

'Oh! You mean they're all separate! And you can put in and take out!'

'Now you've got it. They're all separate till you put them together on another tape. And that's called the mix.'

'Dear Arthur. We went' – she crossed out *we* and put *I*–'to a famous beach called Bondi. I liked the way the women drivers brought the big buses swooping down the hill to the ocean.' The tops of old buildings, the upper window frames that I see from the bus are all rotten and peeling. Things rot up here. It must be the sea air. Even the hotel we are staying in is rotting away. I looked down from our window and saw a big rat browsing on a rubbish heap. It is the kind of hotel where people leave their doors open and when you pass a room you see a pair of bare feet sticking out off the end of the bed. In the street the thin girls call to the passing men: 'Wanna girl?' In the afternoon a damp wind springs up and tears through the alleys that separate the buildings. Sometimes there is a storm. Clouds hang down in lurid loops, like a sagging ceiling. I have washed my white shirt and hung it in the open window. The wind makes it flap like a ghost: in the damp air things take longer to dry. On the bus I saw a tiny baby. Its mother lifted it to her shoulder without properly supporting its head: up it came, blind, its chin quivering violently. I walk round the city. I look at pictures, I look at the water. I went to a photo exhibition and saw a picture of a black man in New York who had just killed someone: he was lying on a bench at the police station with his head in a woman's lap, and his face was quite peaceful. I was walking through Martin Place and I said good morning to an old woman who was selling flowers. She looked at me coldly and when I got past her she laughed. She went *her her her*. She was laughing at me. 'Don't forget to rinse the chlorine out of your bathers every time you get back from the baths. When I come home I will bring you a present. Lots of love, Mum.'

❖

They took the cocaine off the flat part of her nail clippers, in a dogleg lane outside a cinema. They strode out of the lane in step.

It was late, in the bar, later than the middle of the night. The girl had frizzy hair and black-rimmed eyes. She smiled at him from further round the bar. She got off her stool, left her friends sitting there, and forced her way through the pack. She inserted herself between Athena and Philip, and began to hug his head and kiss his forehead.

'What's your name?' said Philip.

'Don't you remember? Angie. Down at the –'

'Yeah, yeah, I remember now.' He kept smiling at her.

'I'm going to the toilet,' said the girl. She staggered away.

He turned straight back to the bar and said, as if to himself, 'I should've followed her out there.'

'What?' said Athena.

'I said, she probably wanted me to follow her out there. But I've, I don't know how to do that stuff any more.'

Athena watched the barmaid. She wore a little peaked yachting cap on the back of her head, and flared canvas pants cut very low and laced back and front to show her pubic hair and the cleft between her buttocks. From the hips up she was naked. She had small firm high pale-nippled teenage breasts. Her face was mild and expressionless. She worked efficiently, filling glasses, taking money, not meeting the eyes of those she served. Her breasts were pretty, they swelled on her ribcage, they were a mild swelling under the skin. Athena gazed at them, and at her unemotional face.

The girl who liked Philip came back from the lavatory. She

[68]

shoved in next to him again and said in a ringing tone, 'We were discussing whether that was Kate Fitzpatrick or not, over there.'

'It is her,' said Athena.

The girl was not listening. She was turned towards Philip. His eyes flashed, he smiled at her, Athena felt his hard left hand pass round the girl's back and brush against her own waist.

'Is it her?' said the girl.

'Must be,' said Philip.

'Yucky guy she's with,' said the girl. 'Yucky, *yucky* guy.'

'It might be her father,' said Athena.

The girl was kissing Philip again. He did not kiss back. He sat there and let her kiss his forehead and the top of his hair. She had her right arm round his neck.

'Is that your boyfriend over there you were with?' he said.

'Him? No. Lovely guy. I've just been in love with someone for a year. Not him. It's over.'

'Did he leave you?' said Philip.

'He was a *beautiful* guy. I really loved him. But hard. Hard as hard as hard.'

'Who's the girl you were with?'

'That's Rowena. My flat-mate.'

'Your flat-mate?'

'Yeah. Gorgeous, isn't she.'

'Very pretty.'

'And not only is she very pretty. She is the nicest, loveliest person you could ever hope to meet.'

She slung her other arm round Athena's shoulders and bent her knees, so that their three heads were on a level at the bar like friends about to have their photo taken. Her arm was heavy, a dead weight.

Philip did not send her away. Athena waited for her to go. In a little while she did. Philip stood up and put his arms round Athena from behind. She turned her head and he kissed her on the lips, a dry kiss.

'I'm glad you're here,' he said. His glance passed her shoulder. His voice was light and toneless. 'I'm glad you said you weren't in love with me. The minute you said that, *I* fell in love with *you*.'

They both felt it, as a passenger in a jet senses the precise moment at which the zenith of its trajectory is reached and passed. It was not the fact of it, but the suddenness that surprised her. She said nothing. She looked at him. A single word occurred in her mind, in Dexter's voice, flat and definite: bullshit. The light in the bar wiped everyone's faces free of lines, of expression, of experience. It was a pink light, an apricot light.

'I think I'll go back to the hotel,' she said.

He looked at her sharply. Which of them had dismissed the other? I will grow old and die, he thought, without moral consolation.

'I'll see you there, then,' he said.

She nodded and walked away.

'If –' he called after her, but she did not hear, and kept walking.

'How did you know where to find me?'

'Morty told me.'

He was thinner. He stood without baggage in the ugly lobby.

'Come home.'

'No. I haven't finished yet.'

'Come home.'

'I can't.'

'Let's go home.'

'I'll never forgive you if you make me.'

'*Make* you? How could I make you? I love you.'

She shrugged. 'At home I was half dead.'

He began to cry. His face twisted, his mouth was lumpy. He gritted his teeth. He would not use the children against her, he would not.

She saw him sob. She did not step closer. If he mentioned them, if he spoke their names, she would splinter. He was afraid of her. She had the stance and the expression of an idiot struck dumb, but an idiot who was holding an axe. He turned and shoved out the door and on to the street.

The night was warm, the air was creamy, the beauty of the city was barbarous. Clumps of light, sprinkles of light moved along dark washes. There were nets of stars; and where there were none, a dense blackness reigned. Dexter walked and wept. Near dawn he found himself in the gardens of an institution. Its upper windows were barred. A smaller, newer building stood apart from the bulk. He went to the open door and looked in. A man in a white cap was shouting under a hanging bulb. Trucks were making deliveries. It was a vast kitchen, lined with metal tanks and vats, comfortless. Here food would be crudely cooked, without love, slung about and loaded on to trolleys for those less fortunate than ourselves. People who had to eat it were surely lost souls.

Athena waited for Philip until she fell asleep. Philip, between the bar and the hotel, encountered a keyboard player of his acquaintance and went with him in his black BMW to a place where music industry people drank and girls prowled. He finished the coke, and a girl, perhaps even the one who had kissed his head in the first bar, went down on her knees to him in a lavatory whose walls jumped and chattered with the secret words of the night.

❖

The back door did not lock: the wood was wormy, the metal loop had lost its grip. Vicki went to the boys' room and fortified herself, as women do, with the sight of sleeping children, the abandonment of limbs, the oblivious breathing, the throats offered to the blade. 'If anyone came to harm them,' thought Vicki, 'I would kill. Without even thinking twice.' Thus, having imbued their limp bodies with her own vulnerability, she felt iron; but took the hammer out of the toolbox and carried it with her to the front room and laid it on the second pillow. She spent a comfortable, contented night alone in the Foxes' double bed. She woke several times and redisposed her limbs and thought, 'How comfortable I am! How contented!' At dawn someone in the house next door slid open a window.

[71]

Vicki sat up and tugged back the curtain. The moon was hidden behind thin, pinkish clouds, and there was a sharp smell of gums. She lay down and turned on the radio, and slipped back into riotous two-dimensional sleep pricked by the elegant needles of a harpsichord. When she woke again in full light the brown hammer looked silly beside her head, like a symbol left behind by a dream. Billy began to shuffle and to wail. She hid the hammer under the sheet and got out of bed.

The piano was shut. The kitchen table was piled with newspapers, the bin was overflowing, the sink was full of greasy saucepans. Slugs had silvered the matting and the chopping board, and had toiled back to their lairs before this hot morning: their whole night had been spent in slow travelling. Vicki opened the cupboard and a rubber glove fell out in a gesture of appeal. She picked it up and pulled it on.

'I am running this house,' said Vicki. 'Who is in charge here? I am, officer. It is going to be a very hot day. I will wash them, I will feed them, I will take them to the pool. I am holding the fort. I am necessary here. For breakfast I will cook tomatoes under the griller.'

She peeled a banana and shoved it into Billy's hand. While he chewed it she picked the crusts of sleep from his eyes. He champed vilely, with open jaws.

'There's piss in his bed,' said Arthur. 'You shouldn't give him anything to drink at night. Three drinks – piss.' He isolated three fingers and held them up. 'Hey Vicki.' He followed her into his bedroom. She smelt it before she reached the bunks. 'Once I saw this movie called *Excalibur*.'

If Dexter had been there he would have said, 'Film, Arthur, not movie. Movie's an Americanism.' She seized the top sheet and whipped it free of the mattress. 'Don't tell me the plot,' she said, 'for God's sake.'

'And there was this mighty sword which had become stuck in a mighty rock, and whoever could manage to pull it out, well he could be the king.'

'I don't want to hear a story, Arthur. I've just woken up.'

'And there was this boy – well, he was a young man really, or a teenager –'

'Shutup, Arthur. I'm busy.'

'– who was befriended by Merlin, the greatest magician the

world had ever known, and he –'

'Will you shut *up*?'

She turned round with her arms full of stinking sheets. He had not heard a word. His eyes had gone out of focus, his pitch was up, his pace was accelerating, his smile was the one-sided, manic grimace of the born raver: he was away on the high seas of narrative. In the wide planting of his feet, his blithe assumption of an audience, she saw Dexter, oh poor Dexter, gone away on a plane to try and pull the sword out of the stone. Her insides quivered with what she thought was laughter. She pushed the chattering boy aside: he turned to follow her, pointed his rapt, jabbering face in her direction, but she stepped out into the passage and closed the door on him. He took no notice: as she walked away his chipmunk voice rattled on without interruption.

She stood among the rank stalks of the tomato plants. Her legs itched and the sun struck through the back of her cotton nightdress. A bird sat on the fence and trilled madly. It spotted her and flipped away across the vegetable patch to a tree, where it threw back its head, opened its beak like a pair of scissors, and sang tune after tune.

'See that boy?' roared Arthur into Vicki's ear. 'Well his name is Dennis Dwyer. He gets the strap all the time. He's a really horrible type of person. Not very bright either.'

The boy strolled up and cast himself on the concrete step above them. His shoulders were blistered and flaking. He looked straight into Vicki's face. 'Hullo miss,' he said.

Vicki smiled at him. Arthur withdrew ten feet and squatted frog-like in his green bathers, dripping and spearing bitter looks at the boy, who got up and darted away into the water.

All afternoon he kept coming back. Each time he lay closer to Vicki, his thin chest heaving, his eyes red with chlorine. He was patiently waiting his turn. When Arthur took Billy to the kiosk, the boy made his move. He lifted his head from his arms and spoke to her.

'Know what?'

'No. What?'

'I haven't got a mum any more.'

'Haven't you?'

'No. I've just got a dad and a nanna.'

'What happened to your mum? Did she d – get sick, and die?'

'She went away.' He sat up and folded his arms round his blue knees. 'And I don't think she's coming back.' He was taking his time.

'Gee. How did your dad feel? Did he get mad? Or upset?'

'Hoo yeah. He says he's gonna shoot her.'

He nudged himself across so that his upper arm was touching hers. They sat parallel; they stared out over the glaring water with its moving threads of light and shadow. Over the boy's head she saw the empty scaffolding of the gasometer: clouds sailed in and out of its framework in great masses, stately and unhurried.

'How do you feel about it? Your mum going away.'

He gave a small turn of the shoulder and shone his face at her for a second. 'Oh – all right. How many kids have you got?'

'Two,' said Vicki.

'I seen the big one at school. Is the other kid yours too?'

'Yes.'

'He's got something wrong with him. Spazzo.'

'Not spastic,' said Vicki. 'Just a bit vague.'

'He's spazzo,' said the boy.

'I haven't got a mother either,' said Vicki.

'What happened to her?'

'Died. Got cancer.'

They went on sitting there. Their arms touched, their knees were drawn up to their chins, their faces grinned into the sun.

'What's the time?' said the boy.

The big clock was exactly opposite them, on the wall of the dressing sheds. 'Just after four,' said Vicki. 'Can't you tell the time?'

'Not on them old kind of clocks.'

Vicki took a bottle of lotion out of her basket, squirted some into her palm, and ran her hand across the boy's shoulders. He

[74]

did not draw away, but presented his whole back to be coated.
The cream disappeared into his skin: his back was the colour of
a burnt stick, his shoulders crackled with broken blisters. The
job done, she took her hand away. Immediately he twisted
round and turned up his face like a plate being offered.

'Look at me scabs.'

'One of them's loose,' said Vicki. She pulled it off his top lip.
He winced with his eyes closed, giving her his face without
defence. His blond hair was sopping, thickened into greenish
matted clumps. Vicki saw the tender stalks of his eyebrows.
'What happened?'

'I come off me bike. Over the handlebars.' He was almost in
her arms, his eyes squeezed shut, his face turned up. Her
basket had been overturned. The pages of her magazine
riffled in a gust of dry wind: her hat brim whirred.

The PA squealed and a man's voice bellowed, 'THAT BOY IN
THE RED BATHERS. STOP YOUR PUSHING. REPORT TO THE
MANAGER'S OFFICE.'

The boy's eyes popped open. He glanced down at himself to
check the colour of his bathers. They were blue. He sprang up
without a backward look and galloped down the high steps to
the water.

The afternoon changed its colour. The wind dropped,
people raised hands to their eyes, the screaming children
paused for breath, the water flattened and turned brassy.
Dexter paid at the turnstile and ploughed through the herd of
dripping midgets.

'Here's Dad!' shrilled Arthur.

There was no-one with him. She must be at home, getting
the tea ready or taking the clothes off the line before it started
to rain. Vicki saw Dexter scoop up Arthur in his arms, saw
Arthur struggle to be put down, panicking lest his friends see
his father treat him like a baby. She kept her hand round Billy's
wrist and waited for news. Dexter seemed to be coming very
slowly towards her, with the twisting boy in his arms. People
were scrambling out of the water and running away to their
towels. The remaining heads, breaking the slate meniscus,
looked like the victims of a massacre.

'Look at that inky sky!' chattered a voice among the group on
the step below her. 'Remember the dust cloud last year? Wasn't

[75]

it awesome when it came over the flats!'

'You could tell this wasn't New York!' said another. 'If that had happened on Manhattan everybody would have been saying *Oh my gahd!* Did you notice? Not one single person said *Oh my gahd!*'

He came up the steep concrete levels to the wall against which she sat, and put Arthur neatly back on to his feet. The boy was red: he hitched up his bathers and turned his back. The dry wind gasped and began again. The girl and the man stared at each other. Dexter's eyes seemed to have darkened and fallen back into his head. Something important is happening in this family, thought Vicki, and I am part of it now, whether I like it or not.

❖

Elizabeth reflustered her wind-flattened hair and examined the cut of her jacket in the reflecting front of the beer fridge. She was pleased. The barman went out the back to look for the Campari, and she picked up off the counter one of those little four-page bulletins on duplicator paper which announce the results of inter-pub darts and pool competitions. There was a joke at the bottom of the page. She read it.

'*Gynaecologist to dentist*: "I don't know how you can stand your job, smelling people's bad breath all day." '

Her legs surprised her: that old, almost forgotten sensation, as if all the blood were draining rapidly out of them, leaving them fragile and chalky, unable to support her. They do hate us, she thought. The weight of disgust that loaded the simple joke made her bones weak. She thought, I can't bear it, I can't. She thought, I should be able to bear it by now. It has just caught me off guard. She thought, Dexter would think it was funny. She screwed up the bulletin and dropped it into the ashtray at her feet.

'Campari,' said the barman, returning. 'Never drunk that. Nice, is it? Italian drink, is it?' He twisted the top of the paper bag into a hard twirl.

She paid him the money and did not speak. When she turned her back to leave he pulled the corners of his mouth down, niddled and noddled his head, and twitched his hips in imitation of a stuck-up walk. There was no way he could have known that her heart, for the thousandth time, felt as if it had turned into a sharp splinter.

There was weirdness in the turbulent air. They all felt it, as they passed the flailing fig tree and came up the hot concrete steps to the kitchen; but Billy was berserk. He struggled, he shrieked, he bit his lips until they bled. When Dexter put him down he flung away and galloped among the chairs, overturning them and cannoning off the fronts of cupboards.

'Can't you do something?' cried Vicki. 'I wish Athena was here!'

'Well she's not,' said Dexter. 'Anyway she can't do anything with him either when he's like this. It's electro-magnetic.'

'Sing to him.'

'I don't feel like singing,' said Dexter. His face was grim. '*You* sing.'

'Me? *I* can't sing.'

The little boy, wailing like a fire engine, was trying to cram himself into the greasy space between the bench and the stove. His shoulder was smeared with dirty fat, his bathers were twisted round his loins and his erect penis showed white and pointed as a fish. The noise in the room was deafening: the chairs crashing and rolling, the thin voice screeching, the hot wind whining through the half-open window. Dexter was stupefied, he was ugly with sadness.

'Do something,' said Vicki.

'There's somebody at the door,' shouted Arthur.

In came Elizabeth, all cool and high-heeled and clean, carrying the bottle in its paper bag and a net sack full of oranges.

'What *is* this?' she called in her piercing, silvery voice. 'This place is a madhouse!'

She put her load on the table, righted the lolling chairs and dragged the roaring boy out of his oily hiding place.

[77]

'Here, you take him,' she said. 'I don't know what to do with kids.'

Dexter snapped out of it. He seized Billy's hands and spun him round, crouched, enfolded him like a foetus in a cage of limbs and torso. The boy was defeated, but he raged and clamoured: he could scream even with his mouth shut, the very bones of his skull were in commotion.

'He's chucking a mental!' cried Vicki.

'Fill up the bath and stick him in it,' said Arthur, calmly colouring in at the table. 'That's what Mum does.'

Vicki ran to turn on the taps.

The boy stopped to draw breath, and the rain started. A mass, a block, a volume of water crashed on to the roof. The temper of the air changed: in some meteorological bureau the dials flicked back to zero. Elizabeth opened the back door and they stood in a row, Dexter with the limp boy over his shoulder, and stared out at the wall of rain.

Elizabeth lined up the knife, the board the squeezer, the glasses, and began to work with easy efficiency. As she sliced she spoke to Dexter over her elegant shoulder.

'So. She wouldn't come back, eh?'

He twisted his head away.

'Come on, Dex. Don't be a drama queen.'

'Think it's funny, do you.'

'She'll be back. Listen to me! I know him. He has the attention span of a stick insect. I'll lay odds she'll be back in a couple of days.'

'And then what happens?'

'That's up to you.'

'Couldn't you have stopped it?' he said.

'What for? It's none of my business.'

'But you must have known what was going on.'

'What if I did? You didn't expect me to dob her, did you? I have got some shreds of feminist loyalty left. Anyway if it hadn't been Philip it would've been someone else.'

'No! It's *his* fault. She was naive. He saw that. He took advantage of her.'

Elizabeth gave a snort of laughter. 'You don't think much of her, do you.'

'She's a saint! Someone like you couldn't even see that!'

'*Someone like me*,' said Elizabeth. 'What's that supposed to mean?'

'I hate the way you talk,' he said, 'and I hate the way you live. Smashing everything. Smash, smash, smash, smash – then what? *Fuck*, you say. Fuck this and fuck that. I even hate the way you pronounce the word.'

'It's a simple word,' she said. 'I'd never even heard it used till I met you. There's not much range available. Fuck. Fewck. Furk.'

'It's the shape of your mouth when you say it. It's blunt. You spit it out.'

They had never fought before. They looked ugly to each other, swollen with the desire to do harm. He was afraid of the way he imagined she lived; and she wanted, in some obscure sadism, to induct him into it, into the rough sexual world that lies outside families.

Vicki heard their voices turn low and nasty. She sang in a whisper to the placid boy in the bath: 'A band of angels comin' after me, Comin' for to carry me home.' It was one of the few songs he would tolerate. She swilled the water up his back in a rhythm, scrubbed at the horny skin of his heels. There was a stoned voluptuousness in his acceptance of her caresses which, if she let herself think about it, made her gorge rise, but still she sang and sloshed the water up and down his unblemished back.

There were heavy steps outside and the bathroom door flew open.

'I'll finish him off,' shouted Dexter.

He cast himself on his knees beside Vicki, took the face washer from her hand and raised his big round voice: 'I'll sing you a song of the fish of the sea – o-oh, Ri-o!'

Vicki, upstaged, scurried away into the kitchen.

A glass jug stood on the table, full of a thick reddish-orange liquid. 'Flash drinks,' said Elizabeth.

'Why do you have to fight with everyone?' said Vicki.

'Me? He started it!'

'You both started it,' said Arthur. 'I don't care if people fight.

I think it's rather interesting, actually.'

'Mister Cool,' said Elizabeth. 'Tiny Tim in the kitchen corner.'

Arthur shot her a flirtatious smile.

'I must say, Arthur,' said Elizabeth, 'you have very spunky legs for a boy of your age.'

'I've got a girlfriend at school,' said Arthur.

'I'm not surprised.'

'Want to see some photos of me when I was a baby?' said the boy. 'I'll go and get them.' He darted out of the room.

'You always con people,' said Vicki.

'I have no shame,' said Elizabeth. 'Let's drink these.'

They began. It was still raining steadily. The room was almost dark.

'Don't you care about Philip and Athena?' said Vicki.

'Course I care. I always care. But there's no point in making a song and dance about it, like that night he stayed here. Know something? There's only one thing that'll bring 'em back, and that's indifference. The one thing you can't fake.'

'But you *are* faking it.'

'At the moment I might be. But as soon as it stops being faked and starts being real, he'll turn up. Rule number one of modern life.'

Vicki shuddered. 'You're cold. You're too detached. You're scary.'

Arthur romped in with a packet. He spread the colour photos out on the scratched table top. Elizabeth bent over them. 'They're rude!' she cried. Arthur skipped about, squint-eyed with laughter. The photos were of a naked baby boy lying on his back like a frog, flashing the enormous, raw genitals of the new-born.

'That's what I get for coming on to yobbos,' said Elizabeth. 'Put them away, you hoon.'

'I bet you're not really shocked,' said Arthur. 'I bet you're only pretending.' He sniggered to himself and gathered up the photos.

'Come on, Vicki,' said Elizabeth. 'Let's get smashed.'

'Hang on,' said Vicki. She separated one of the photos from the slippery pile. 'Who's this?'

It was a picture of two men standing in a garden so green

that it could not have been in Australia, the kind of green that to Vicki's untravelled eye looked like a trick of the camera: a deep, lolling, effortless green without even a tinge of yellow.

'Is that Dexter?' said Vicki.

Elizabeth tilted her chair to look. 'It is. It's Dexter and his father. In London. That must've been taken nearly twenty years ago. My Gahd. Will you look at that suit he's got on. The seams are all lumpy. It could do with a good press. That boy always did look a sight.'

The older man, Vicki saw, stood side-on, as if about to slip out of frame: his smile was crooked, almost sly. But Dexter! Dexter faced the camera with a frank, cheerful look. His hands were plunged deep in his trouser pockets. His hair was shockingly blond: it sprang back off his high, narrow, unlined forehead. He was young. A teenager. An HSC student. Hardly older than herself. He was not afraid of the camera, of the world. He liked the world, and he expected the world to like him. What was the word for the quality that shone in his plain, open face? It was *goodness*.

'You know, Vicki,' said Elizabeth, 'you've got to go back to school in February. You've got to study.'

'You didn't,' said Vicki. She slipped the photo under a newspaper.

'I did so! I went to university.'

'You never got your diploma.'

'Degree is the word.'

'Degree, graduated, whatever it's called.'

'No, but I studied.'

'I bet you didn't study any more than you had to.' Vicki guzzled her drink. 'I bet I know what you did at uni. You fucked.'

Arthur let out a high-pitched giggle.

'You should talk,' said Elizabeth. 'And don't call it uni. Only people who've never been there call it that.'

'What's for tea?' said Arthur.

'We're drinking,' said Elizabeth. 'We're getting drunk. Why don't you cook something?'

'I'm hungry,' he said, with more force.

'Eat some cheese.'

Vicki laughed, and drank. Arthur thought for a moment.

His eyes slid to the closed bathroom door. 'Billy will be hungry too when he comes out of there,' he said. 'He'll be absolutely starving. And he can't cook.'

'But you could,' said Elizabeth. She turned her full attention on him, and he rose to it.

'But I don't know how to.'

'But you could if you tried.'

'But my mother never taught me.'

'But I can teach you.'

'But you're not my mother.'

'But I can still teach you.'

'But I'm not allowed to turn on the gas.'

'But I can turn it on for you.'

'But I might burn myself.'

'But I'll rub Savlon on your wounds.'

'But fat might splash in my eye and make me go blind.'

'But I'll get you a guide dog.'

'But we haven't got a kennel for a blind dog.'

'But he can sleep beside your bed.'

'But he might piss on the floor.'

'But you can clean it up in the morning.'

'But Mum won't like it.'

'But she's not here, so she won't find out.'

They stopped on a rising note. Dexter was standing in the bathroom doorway, holding Billy by the hand, lit from behind through a cloud of metallic steam.

'Some things, Morty,' he said, 'strain a person's sense of humour.'

He swept through the room. The three of them sat foolishly, with fading smiles. It was dark, and the rain had stopped. Vicki stood up and switched on the lamp in the corner: the disorder of the room, its stuffiness and neglect, would have made her feel guilty had she not been already half drunk: as it was, she witnessed minor twinges of the appropriate emotions occurring distantly, as if to some other girl in a similar circumstance. She pushed her glass across the table to her sister, who filled it again without meeting her eye.

By the time Dexter splashed down the sideway with the pizza boxes on his fore-arms, Elizabeth was setting the table. He stopped to wipe his feet and saw the big, free, two-handed gesture with which she flung out the tablecloth, a movement which seemed to him so carelessly proprietary, so symbolic of serene domesticity, that performed by someone other than his mother or his wife, parodied indeed by this viper, it became a travesty of truth and beauty. And yet the face she turned to him when she heard his feet scraping the mat was softened by the flush of alcohol: in the inadequate light she looked younger, sorrier, more deferential, more as he preferred to remember her.

Vicki was trying to find music on the radio. 'I'll turn it off, Dex,' she said, 'if you don't feel up to it.'

'No, leave it,' he said. He held out the boxes to Elizabeth and sat down. 'That's Berlioz. Leave that on.'

'Opera,' said Elizabeth under her breath. She opened the cutlery drawer and scrabbled among the metal.

The announcer, a young and bashful man whose tentative voice could have reached the airwaves only on an amateur station, began to read out a synopsis.

'In the next act,' he murmured, 'Margaret waits for Faust. She waits and waits, but in vain: he does not come. He is in the depths of the forest, invoking Nature.'

The sisters glanced at each other over Dexter's head. Elizabeth laid one hand over her heart and raised the other in a gesture of tremendous romantic suffering. 'Invoking nature!' she mouthed. But Vicki would not laugh. She stood in the middle of the room, not knowing what to do with her hands, and looked uncertainly at Dexter. Her face was blurred. She's drunk, thought Elizabeth. And so am I. She lowered her arm and set five places on the cloth. Dexter was sitting quite still between the children, looking down at the curl of steam that rose from the round hole in the pizza box. He was listening to the music.

Elizabeth lifted the lid off the pizza. Everyone sat forward. They ate in their fingers. If there is a spectre at this feast, thought Elizabeth, I'm it. She saw that though she had been able to bring a momentary order to this room, putting things in piles and clearing a space for action, she had not cleaned it, or made it into what they were all waiting for. Its surfaces were dull with the absence of meaning. The house itself was waiting.

She took a taxi to Philip's house. Poppy was asleep against the cushions with the phone beside her and an exercise book still open on her knee. 'It's dark and smoky in the Paradise Cafe,' she had written. 'You order a coffee, and you get it straight away. You can't eat croissants at the Paradise Cafe. But you get good coffee for the price you pay.'

Elizabeth turned on the television and sat down. It was an old French movie, half over. She wondered if she could dress like one of those maids, and trot about in high-heeled shoes with a strap across the instep, in a little fitted black dress to the knee and white collar and cuffs. She would need thin French lips, eyebrows plucked to a fine line, black curls over her forehead, and a piercing voice, sharp as the tinkling of her mistress's silver bell. A maid: but whom should she serve?

When the film ended a Greek man explained in his native tongue the details of the government's health scheme. It took him fully ten minutes, with diagrams, and then an Italian came on and repeated the performance in his language. Elizabeth watched and listened. She recognised a word here and there. It was soothing, this patient setting out of facts and services. She picked up Poppy's legs and arranged them across her lap. The tendons behind the girl's knees tightened like wires. 'You smell nice,' murmured Poppy. 'This lovely smell.' A choir of old people in blue robes sang to close down the station. It was a Jewish choir. 'In joyful strains then let us sing, Advance Australia Fair!'

[84]

Vicki began to talk. She held her head in her two hands, but was in danger of dropping it among the pizza crusts: it swayed, her elbows were too pointy, the table was too wooden. She had a lot of things she needed to say to Dexter. She was not sure whether he was paying attention; from time to time he did not seem even to be in the room, but then she would swing her head round and find him still sitting opposite her, looking at her from a long way away. The boys had gone. Someone must have put them to bed.

'I hated it when she came home for visits. They fought and fought, and Mum used to cry in the bathroom. After she died I used to think I would get sick too. Elizabeth said I was a hypochondriac, but *I* said at the doctor's they just look on your card and if you're a hypochondriac it shows. Let's make another one of those drinks. Where's Elizabeth.'

'She went hours ago. I'm going to put you to bed now. Come on. Can you stand up?'

'Yes. I can.' She could, and did, with skill. 'I can put myself to bed.' She walked to the door. 'What about the washing up?'

'Go to bed.'

'Goodnight.' She came slowly back to the table and held out her hand to shake his. 'Goodnight, Dexter. I have enjoyed our conversation.' He put out his hand and she pumped it vigorously. She laughed. 'And now you're supposed to say "What soft hands you have! All the better to touch you with!" '

'Go to bed.'

'They should be bloody soft, what with all the cream I put on them every day! They are soft, aren't they?'

'Very soft. Go to bed.'

'I'm going, I'm going. Now you have to say "God bless you. Sleep tight. Sweet dreams." That's what my mother used to say. Did you ever see my mother?'

'Yes. I danced with her at Morty's twenty-first.'

'Did you? I was only a baby then. You didn't know me then, did you?'

'I saw you. I was allowed to hold you.'

'Did Athena?'

'No. I didn't know Athena then.'

She let go his hand and backed away.

'I'll bring you a bucket,' said Dexter.

'What for?'

'In case you chuck in the night.'

She stared at him, and blundered out the door.

The buckets in the bathroom all had underclothes soaking in them. He emptied one lot out into the basin and carried the dripping bucket into Vicki's room. She had not taken off her clothes; she was lying on top of the sheet. Her eyes were open and the overhead light was on.

'If I shut my eyes,' she said, 'I get the whirling pit *so bad*.'

'Shouldn't you drink a couple of glasses of water?' he said. She made no response. He folded two pillows and wedged them under her neck, to keep her head upright. Her feet were bare, and the gap between her big toe and the next one was ingrained with grey dirt. He pulled up a blanket and spread it over her.

'Night,' she sang. 'Ni-ight.'

Damn braces; bless relaxes. Dexter could not utter the words God bless you. She had forgotten him, anyway. He stood with his hand on the light switch and looked at the small hump she made under the blanket. He did not know which of the two of them was the more pathetic. He tiptoed out of the room and turned off the light behind him.

On his way through the kitchen he screwed up the pizza boxes and tried to force them into the stuffed bin, but they would not go so he left them standing in the corner. He shuffled the newspapers into a pile and his fingers slid across the cold surface of a photo. He picked it up and looked at it with dull eyes. Green. The boy, the young man was smiling in the garden, and the father was walking away.

'*The blushing apricot, and woolly peach*,' said Dexter, '*Hang on thy walls, that every child may reach.*'

Vicki's eyes rolled up, and closed. The room lurched into motion, the bed tilted, there was a shallow rapid panting. Each pore squeezed out an icy droplet. She fell and fell, backwards through the universe, and the starry emptiness above her shrank to a circle the size of a plughole, and when that went out she would be dead. Her ears were full of a stellar drone, her jaws ran with spit. She flung herself sideways and the bucket edge dug into her cheek.

Somebody stood in the doorway, somebody came in in the dark. Somebody weighed the bed down and put his arms round her, and held her head and wiped her mouth.

'Don't, don't let me,' she babbled.

'Don't what?'

'Don't let me fall asleep. If I go to sleep I'll die. I don't want to, don't let me.'

❖

Athena woke at six o'clock in the morning. Philip was not there, nor had he been. The room was full of heavy, dark pieces of furniture. The impression that her presence made on the room was so slight that the turbulence of its former occupants, of a great line of passing strangers, swarmed and tumbled about her in its stuffy atmosphere: their boredom, their panic, their trembling fantasies: wire coat-hangers, shoes with worn-down heels, jumpers smelling of men's sweat, trousers too long or too short for the fashion, bras with greying straps, skirts whose hems dipped at one side. She pulled back the curtains and expected them to fall apart in her hands.

The street was brightening. She heard the sharp clack of a woman's heels, and looked down. The woman was wearing a shapeless dress and carried two plastic supermarket bags. She stopped in front of the closed grille of a shop. She had her back to Athena. She put down one bag, as if to get out a key. Athena did not want to be seen watching. She got back under the sheet. She heard the heels again: the woman was walking away.

What do I know about him? He cleans his teeth standing upright and looking himself straight in the eye in the mirror. Oh, I've never *seen* him clean his teeth. I know this is how he does it because there is a splattering of drops of dried toothpaste all over the bottom half of the mirror. Now I come to think of it, this means he must do it in a slightly bent posture. He is tall. If he did it upright, he would spray the top of the mirror.

She would wait, and see.

At eight o'clock she passed quickly through the lobby, keeping her eyes straight ahead, but she thought the girl at the desk gave her a smart look. She stood in the street outside the hotel. A warm wind was sweeping the grit away: the pavements shone like bone.

What do tourists do? They walk, they stand, they look, they buy. They fumble for money on buses, not knowing whether to pay the driver or the conductor. They visit famous monuments, fountains, old houses full of stone and shutters and anachronistic lace. They notice that the day without duty passes with the slowness of a dream. They know that their existence is without point. They envy those who go arm in arm, who have a home to go to.

In the art gallery she saw a painting of a woman in a dress like molten metal. All she could bear to look at were head portraits and domestic still lives. She looked for pictures of rooms, of windows, of light coming in through windows, of tables on which sat utilitarian objects, of people sitting at tables, of people busy on humble matters. She stopped in front of a painting called *Reading Woman*: she sat in her bonnet inside a room, turning her book towards the window through the top panes of which (the bottom ones being shuttered) fell a splash of yellow light on to the floor at her feet. The floorboards were wide. Three oranges in a tin dish sat on a chair. In the foreground two big pink shoes lay at cast-off angles on the floor.

She walked on and on, until she came to the railway station and bought herself a ticket home.

In the afternoon she went out on the sparkling water to the zoo, and stood for half an hour watching gangs of very small monkeys as bald and as serious as businessmen marching about their rocky enclosure. From there she turned and looked back across the water at the bridge. On its summit wriggled a tiny flag. A man standing near her said to his daughter, 'I bet when they finished building it they all sat round the table feeling excited, and someone said, "*I* know what. How about we stick a little flag right on the very top?"

And the others said, "All right!" '

Just as the sky turned green she passed the conservatorium, white as an ocean liner, with its two high palm trees flying like flags. She stopped on the slope of the lawn and stared up at the lighted first-floor windows: they were open, and three students, each in a separate room, were practising: a piano, a violin, a clarinet. The threads of melody, never meant to combine, mingled and made a pleasant, meaningless discord.

She walked down the neon streets, and up again, and found her way back to the hotel. It was dark.

He was lying on the bed watching a band on television. A girl was sitting at the dressing table, also watching, a spiky girl in a black and white houndstooth dress. Athena spoke from the door.

'I'm going home tonight.'

He sat up with a jerk. 'Come in,' he said, as if she were a visitor. 'Athena, this is . . . ummm . . . She's been showing me a song she wrote.'

'I was just going,' said the girl. The music was very loud. All these songs, thought Athena, are about the end of love, or its wrong beginnings.

'Hang on,' said Philip. 'Excuse me, Athena. Listen. I like your song. Look, I'll give you a tip. Go home and write it again. Take out the clichés. Everybody knows "It always happens this way" or "I went in with my eyes wide open". Cut that stuff out. Just leave in the images. Know what I mean? You have to steer a line between what you understand and what you don't. Between cliché and the other thing. Make gaps. Don't *chew* on it. Don't explain everything. Leave holes. The music will do the rest.'

The girl nodded and nodded. She backed towards the door, keeping her eyes on his face. Athena stood aside for her and she ducked out into the passage and ran away.

'Where have you been all day?' said Philip. 'I waited for you. Let's go out and eat.'

'I'm going on the train. Tonight.'

'Wait another couple of days. We'll fly back.'

She shook her head. The music stopped and the screen was filled with the smiling face of a young man. 'Course,' said the man, the boy, 'an album's a major statement of where a band's at creatively.'

'Aren't you being a bit iron-clad?' said Philip. He swung his feet to the floor. 'It's because I didn't come back last night, isn't it.'

'Dexter came looking for me.'

'Here?' He laughed, and turned off the television. 'Bloody Elizabeth. Big-mouth.'

'I sent him away. He was crying.'

He bent his knees in front of the mirror and flicked his hair about. 'I can't help you with that one, Athena,' he said. 'Jealousy. You'll have to handle that one on your own, I'm afraid.'

He straightened up and faced her. They were like two ghosts, now that the blood had gone out of them, two empty sets of garments hung opposite each other in a cupboard.

'Of *course*,' said Athena. 'Of course I know that. I only came back to get my bag.'

Are there longer nights than those spent sitting up in a second-class seat between Sydney and Melbourne?

At dawn her own reflection receded from the glass, the train groaned and halted, and she looked out at the basalt plain, the striding power lines, the nodding thistles. The landscape was sheep-coloured. Sheep thronged by dams and under trees. The sky was clear. Someone at the front of the carriage turned on a radio, and in the stillness of the sleeping train, before hoarse voices could cry to it to shutup, she heard the music begin again, the whine, the false drama, the seductive little whispering of despair.

Dexter turned over in a muck sweat. There was somebody else in the bed. It was not Athena. But he had his arm around this person. She had her back against his stomach and his hand covered a small, hard breast. A whiff of vomit hung about her hair.

He sprang away to the edge of the bed. She did not move. He crouched there with his feet on the bare boards and his

elbows between his knees. The hugeness of what had happened, of what he had done, fell on him like a haystack: the light
went orange, the air was full of stalks and dust, and then there
was no more air. He got up and stumbled out to the kitchen.

So he was as bad as the rest after all. He was just another
exploiter. He was no better than that tattooed, guitar-playing
turd who'd pushed her up against the fridge and then turned
around and taken Athena away. The feminists were right. Men
were bastards. *He* was a bastard, a low, rotten perv, a slimy
seducer of children. He was practically in loco parentis. He had
abused Morty's trust. He had broken faith with Athena. He
was like one of those men his father made old-fashioned jokes
about: he had let a girl get drunk and then he had taken
advantage of her. And what if she was pregnant? What if she
had to have an abortion? What if that deadshit had given her
the clap and now she'd passed it on to him? He felt this one act
spinning out its consequences forever into infinity. He felt
himself going off the deep end. He went to the sink and made
himself drink off a couple of glasses of water.

The boys must be awake. What if Arthur went into the
bedroom and saw her lying there where his mother was supposed to be? He ran to their room to head them off.

They were lying quietly in their bunks. Billy was singing in
his high, vague voice, a sound more like whistling than singing,
and Arthur was up on one elbow reading with such fierce
intensity that he did not even notice his naked father in the
doorway. The small room was full of sunshine: its window,
closed, was too bright to be looked at, and the air was fuggy
with the smell of children.

'Dexter!'

It was her. He crept away, back into the front room. She was
sitting up in the tangled sheets.

'I dreamed about you,' she said. She was giggling. 'I dreamed
you died. And at the funeral I had on a black dress without a
petticoat and everyone could see my pants.'

'Vicki,' he said. 'I think you'd better get up. Straight away.'
Daylight changed everything. Her breasts grew so high on her
ribcage that he could not help staring at them. 'Quickly. Before
the kids come in here.'

'But I need more sleep,' she said crossly.

[91]

'Get up. Get up.' He whipped the top sheet away.

'I think I'm gonna be sick again.'

She trotted away to the back door and he stripped the bed like a professional. He took the sheets down the back steps and thrust them into the old washing machine under the porch. He had no idea how to make it fill up. He tried to read the instructions on the scratched dial. He realised that he was standing in his back yard with no clothes on, and that a naked teenage girl who was vomiting in the lavatory would emerge at any minute on to the concrete path in full view of any neighbour who cared to stick his head over the fence.

He hid in his bedroom until he heard her shut the bathroom door and turn on the water. It was Sunday morning. Someone in the street was pushing a handmower. The smell of the cut grass seemed to belong to some other, better world that he had shut himself out of. For a moment the rhythmic gnashing of the blades and the distant pounding of the shower covered a smaller, more human sound. Was she *crying*? He dragged on some garments out of the dirty clothes basket and sneaked back into the kitchen.

She was not crying. She had her radio in there with her and she was singing with it: the voice, a man's but pitched high enough for a girl to sing comfortably in the same register, and taking itself very seriously, sang, 'Oh, I'm the kind of guy/Who is always o-o-on the –' He could not catch the last word. The radio and the girl sang with a light, slow, sure rhythm. 'Wherever I lay my hat/That's – my home.' Her voice came and went in clarity and volume: he imagined her turning, bending, raising one arm and then the other, standing with a blind smile under the stream of water. He felt his heartbeat slow down.

Out she came, splendid as the Queen of Sheba, wreathed in pink steam, wet-headed, and wrapped in a threadbare towel. He held his breath for the moral crisis.

She smiled at him. 'I bet I lost half a stone with all that spewing,' she said. 'See how my hip bones are sticking out? I look fabulous! But boy, have I got a headache.'

'Vicki. Listen. I feel terrible about last night.'

'Oh, I know. I must have been foul.'

She rubbed herself with the rag of a towel. Her bottom was flushed, her flesh was so new and firm that even vigorous movement did not make it jiggle.

'No – I mean *I* feel terrible. About what I did.'

She was not even listening. 'I get this thing, you know? where I think I'm going to die if I fall asleep? Must be a neurosis or something. You were really nice to me.'

'Nice?' The young savage, thought Dexter. I am as irrelevant as a missionary. I am being ridiculous. 'But we'll have to tell Athena, of course,' he said.

She looked up. 'What? Don't be stchoopid. It was just a one-night stand. We're not in love, or anything! I'm not, anyway.' She gave a gay laugh and put one foot up on a chair to dry it. 'You can tell her if you *like*. But it might make her feel worse. Like a sort of punishment for going away.'

He had nothing to say.

'Anyway,' said Vicki, 'Athena can hardly complain. That would be hypocritical.'

He sat at the ravaged table and watched the girl dry herself with efficient strokes, sawing between her toes and twisting her shoulders to reach the backs of her thighs. This was modern life, then, this seamless logic, this common sense, this silent tit-for-tat. This was what people did. He did not like it. He hated it. But he was in its moral universe now, and he could never go back.

❖

She walked down the sideway. The car was not there. There was nobody home. The windows were closed, the kitchen was airless, the bathroom floor was flooded, the sink was greasy, the table was piled with papers and dirty plates, the rubbish bin overflowed in the corner, and pizza boxes, screwed into stiff wands, lay around it. Athena put down her bag and walked from door to door. In Vicki's room she smelled vomit. The children's room was still warm. The big bedroom had been stripped and the mattress was half off its base.

She opened the front door and sat down on the step. The cement was dry and already hot. She watched ants crawling over the hose. She noticed that the window panes of the house opposite reflected events which were not taking place in the quiet street: the passing of a truck, of a car, of a bunch of cyclists. She thought carefully about this, turning her head, and worked out that the housefront opposite must be tilted at such an angle that its windows reflected the highway half a mile away, behind her own house, beyond the creek.

She got up and started work.

She opened every window and every door. She carried the newspapers and the pizza boxes down to the bottom of the yard and lit a fire in the incinerator. She turned on the taps of the washing machine and poked the sheets down into the water. She stood in the rubbish bins, trampled their contents down, and lugged them up to the street for tomorrow's collection. She filled a bucket with boiling water and scrubbed the hardened food dribbles off the cupboard doors. She washed, she washed, she washed. She tended the incinerator, and when the fire burned low she kept it going with hunks of wormy timber that she wrenched off the disused rabbit cage. She did load after load of washing, and hung it out to dry. She plunged her hands into the lavatory and carved its stains away. She mopped the kitchen floor and covered it with sheets of newspaper. She got down on her hands and knees and scraped the mould out of the shower and tugged clumps of hair out of the plughole. She emptied the fridge and set a pan of boiling water inside its ice-clogged freezer. The sheets dried so quickly in the sunny back yard that before she had finished the cleaning she was able to remake the beds and tuck them in tightly. The bedrooms smelled of cotton. Every kitchen surface was dry and bare. She picked up the newspapers from the clean lino and took them out to the incinerator, over which a blast of molten air quivered: the leaves of the nectarine tree jumped and wavered in its colourless exhalation. She could hear Mister and Missus Fuckin' cursing each other behind the fence. Their inarticulate croakings were punctuated by the blows of a hammer and the explosions of the flywire door.

She ironed a cloth and spread it on the kitchen table.

And then she sat down and waited for them to come home.

And they will come!

And Vicki will say, as they drive in through the gateway,

'Hey! The bins are out! Athena must be back.'

And Billy will not even have noticed her absence, and Arthur will come and stand beside her, trying not to smile, and Vicki and Dexter will not touch her straight away,

and the clothes on the line will dry into stiff shapes which loosen when touched,

and someone will put the kettle on,

and from one day to the next Poppy will stop holding Philip's hand: he will drop his right hand to her left so she can take it, but nothing will happen, and when he looks down she will be standing there beside him, watching for a gap in the traffic, and she will not hold his hand any more, and she never will again,

and Dexter will sit on the edge of the bed to do up his sandals, and Athena will creep over to him and put her head on his knee, and he will take her head in his hands and stroke it with a firm touch,

and the tea will go purling into the cup,

and Athena will dream again and again, against her will, of Philip, or rather of not-Philip, of searching for him, of climbing endless stairs in a building full of rooms whose occupants have just quitted them, leaving warm cushions and sunny floors and disturbed air,

and Elizabeth and Vicki and Athena will go to visit Como House, they will go arm in arm through the high rooms, and will stoop to examine the inlay tables, the angle of flush in the pink and white marble,

and as they approach the Paradise they will feel the city shudder under the soles of their feet, and will see the heavy strands of the fly curtain swing out on a gust of air, and will hear the soft laughter and the slide of dancing shoes on the speckled concrete, and oh! the machine will be hissing, the tables will be clean, the sun will be shining through the glass,

and Athena will play Bach on the piano, in the empty house, and her left hand will keep up the steady rocking beat, and her right hand will run the arpeggios, will send them flying, will toss handfuls of notes high into the sparkling air!